BRANDING BARON

STELLA WILLIAMS

SERPENTINE CREATIVE LLC

Edited by

Ali Williams – Line Edits

Mandy Smith – Copy Edits and Proofreading – Raw Books Editing

Cover by GermanCreative on Fiverr.com

Contents

CONTENT WARNINGS

This book contains themes related to depression, emotional abuse (not from male lead), animal violence, references to child loss and infidelity.

Chapter One

Baron Cross was glad to be back in familiar territory. The open skies broken only by the moon-kissed peaks of the Sowell Gate Mountains in the distance were the breath of fresh air he needed after being forced to spend the last week in Mulberry with only carefully planned city agricultural spaces to appease his need for the outdoors. He'd barely been able to enjoy even that much as he'd spent most of it in his cousin Elias' legal offices going back and forth with Christine and her lawyers. After three days of hell settling his divorce from his ex, he was finally free. He couldn't wait to get home and celebrate the good news with his family. Christine was out of their lives for good. She'd fought tooth and nail to stay in his life, or rather to have access to his bank account. It had taken two years, and more money than Baron wanted, to finally be rid of the biggest mistake of his life.

Everyone had tried to warn him about Christine, even her own family, but Baron hadn't listened. He'd been too in lust, too excited about being a father, and too responsible to let his first child be born out of wedlock. He'd ignored all the red flags, including her spending habits.

The result? He'd wasted six years with a woman he didn't love. Looking back now, he didn't know why he'd waited so long to end things. Maybe he just didn't want to be the asshole who broke things off so soon after losing their son. Perhaps he'd just been so desperate for any form of comfort at that point. Their son hadn't survived, and that had wrecked them both. He'd gone to therapy, and she'd gone to an expensive treatment facility, but by the time he'd realized their issues went way beyond the devastating loss of a child, it was already years too late.

Baron yawned. He needed to get his car and start making the drive to Edgewood. Sowell City was the closest airport, but Edgewood and his family estate were on the other side of the Sowell Gate Mountains, about a two-hour drive through the city and into the mountains.

When Baron yawned again, he shook his head. So much for sleeping in his own bed tonight. One more night in a hotel room wouldn't kill him like trying to make the drive through the pass while exhausted just might. Baron would check into a hotel for the night and make the drive in the morning. That way, he could make it safely home in the morning in time for his mother's famous Saturday morning waffles. With a smile on his face, Baron decided that sounded like the perfect way to start off his new life. Well rested and with a plate full of golden-brown deliciousness.

On the way to his car, Baron spotted a young woman staring at the transit map by the door, a large hiking backpack on the ground at her feet. He couldn't see her face, but judging by the way she stood with her hands on her hips, she was trying to figure out when the next bus would be by. It was too late for public transit, and the last bus from the airport into the city would have left at least an hour before. Baron should have made the casual observation and kept moving, but for the first time in years, his brain allowed him to appreciate the woman's voluptuous curves.

She was on the shorter side, with nice thick curves that filled every inch of the denim of her jeans. The pale blue cotton of her t-shirt felt a little too cool for the golden undertones of the sliver of skin revealed just above the waist of her jeans. They molded to her form in a way that made his fingers itch to peel the layers away and reveal more of her tantalizing features. He allowed himself to wonder if her curves would feel as soft in his hands as they looked, if she would mind his hands in her thick kinky curls as he buried his face in the crook of her neck, or better yet, if her hands would bury into his hair while he sank his tongue between her legs. The woman shifted her weight from her right leg to the left. Her hips followed suit, and the resulting pose highlighted the fullness of her backside. Baron's dick twitched in his pants, and he found himself shifting his own weight as he readjusted himself.

Get a grip, man. You know none of that is going to happen.

Baron was a man of his word and hadn't touched another woman since he'd married, not even during the divorce. Now that it was final, his libido would not let him stay a monk for much longer. That didn't mean he needed to forget every bit of decency he had left and openly lust after a strange woman at the airport.

Christine's only been out of your life for a few hours. The last thing you need is to be a total creep at the airport.

The internal chastisement was enough to refocus Baron on his priorities. He could get back into the dating scene later at the appropriate time and with the appropriate scenario of meeting someone. Right now, he needed to focus on getting home so he could take the final steps in his plan to undo all the damage Christine had wrought in his life.

Still, he wasn't a complete asshole. The woman obviously could use some guidance.

"You'll need to call a cab. Public transit doesn't run this late," Baron called over to her.

The woman jumped and spun around. "Shit, you scared the mess out of me."

If her body hadn't already jump-started his libido, her cherub-cheeked face, with its thick pouty lips and wide brown eyes framed by thick feathery lashes, would have been more than enough to fuel any man's X-rated fantasies.

"Sorry, I was just trying to help," he said and started to walk away.

"Wait! Are you headed into Sowell City too? Mind if we split a cab?" she asked.

Baron groaned. He should say no and wish her goodnight, but his mother's lessons in gentlemanly behavior were hard to shake. He couldn't leave her alone this late at night in case cab drivers chose to stay closer to town to catch the late-night bar crowd. Especially when he knew another man might come along. One with far less self-control and reasons to leave the girl be than Baron had.

Right. You are just the ultimate gentleman, and it has nothing to do with the fact that she's gorgeous.

"Actually, I'm from around here. My name is Baron, and I can give you a ride into town."

The woman bit her lower lip, as if considering her options. Baron waited patiently, studying the row of perfect white teeth that made tiny indentations on her lips. Indentations his tongue suddenly wished to soothe.

"Thank you, Baron. That would be nice," she said, breaking into Baron's thoughts.

He blinked a few times, caught off guard and embarrassed that he'd probably been staring like a lech. Then her words finally sunk in, and his embarrassment quickly faded to a feeling of excitement. She'd accepted his offer of a ride.

Baron smiled and reached for her pack. "Let me help you with that..."

"Genesis," she said and handed him her bag.

She watched him as he registered the weight of the deceptively light-looking bag. Thankfully, Baron hadn't let his depression keep him out of the gym. Otherwise, he'd look a plum fool struggling with her stuff. The fact that he was able to lift it without straining or making a face seemed to engender some goodwill with Genesis because she smiled and gestured for him to lead the way. Baron's truck wasn't the newest model, nor was it flashy in any way. Hell, it was primer blue and older than he was.

He'd never been ashamed of his ride before, no matter how much Christine had nagged him about it. Yet, now he was seeing the vehicle with new eyes. When he'd been younger, girls only cared that he had a car, not how nice it looked. Women his age now would see this car and probably run in the other direction. He cast a quick glance over at the woman to see what her reaction would be, if she would suddenly decide she would wait for a cab instead.

"She might not look pretty, but I promise she's reliable," Baron said.

The woman looked up and smirked at him. "She?"

Baron frowned, unsure of how to answer that or even if he should. Instead, he just shrugged his shoulders and opened the door for her. She climbed in, shaking her head. Baron felt like he was missing something as the sudden urge to get on the road and away from the woman overcame him.

He had a feeling that the longer he was in her presence, the more intertwined their fates would be. The sensation was unwelcome but not unfamiliar. He'd had similar feelings happen to him in the past. Baron's intuition was one he'd gotten used to ignoring, and it had always led to his detriment. However, his gut feeling about Genesis was different in that it wasn't dread or uncertainty that twisted and cramped in his stomach but a gentle fluttering, an overwhelming calm mixed with the thrill of adventure.

Maybe once he got home, he'd make another visit to his Aunt Mirna, the family's self-proclaimed witch. He'd never admit it to his brothers, but he'd even gone to see his Aunt Mirna just before he'd caught Christine cheating on him. He'd felt sick to his stomach when Christine had left on that particular trip, and the feeling had nagged him for days before he'd gone to his aunt to see if it was more than just the average gut feeling. Aunt Mirna's eye-opening concoction had been full of hallucinogens. Baron had not been prepared for the intensity of the experience. The crazy shit he'd seen not only confirmed his fears about Christine but also the family lore about half-human, half-animal creatures in the Sowell Gate Forest. There was no way he'd ever admit to believing in the family lore after the way he'd ruthlessly teased his youngest brother Bechet for doing so. The details of that interaction would forever be a secret between the two of them. But it had confirmed that his gut feelings weren't something to ignore.

The familiar wave of sadness threatened to overcome Baron, and he took a moment to breathe through it before tossing both his luggage and her backpack into the back. There was no point in falling down that rabbit hole any further. What happened in his past was just that, in his past. Right now, he needed to focus on the future, and it was already too late for him to change the course of things with regard to the stunning Ms. Genesis. He rounded the vehicle to slide into the driver's seat. It was only then that he realized he might need to offer the girl some reassurance before driving off with her.

Genesis sat in the passenger seat, holding her hands awkwardly in her lap as if the two minutes sitting alone in his car were enough for her previous self-assured behavior to evaporate. This only confirmed his suspicions.

"Sowell City is bigger than most people think. I promise I'm not trying to be all in your business. I would just like to make sure you arrive safely at your destination. You can even snap a picture of me and send it to a friend if that will make you feel better."

Genesis looked up with a smirk. "Oh, I've already done that. You didn't notice me take a snap of your license plate earlier?"

Baron smiled back. "No, I was a little preoccupied."

"Oh, I bet," she said, running her gaze up and down his body.

Baron knew he was woefully out of practice with flirting, but it still bothered him not being able to tell if Genesis was checking him out or eyeing him with suspicion. Then again, if she truly thought he was up to no good, she would never have gotten into his run-down truck in the first place. She stopped her perusal by meeting his eyes, and Baron swore he saw a flash of gold in her eyes before she quickly turned to face the window away from him.

Baron forced his gaze away and cleared his throat. "Well, I guess we should hit the road." When she didn't answer but instead pulled out her phone, Baron took that as his cue that she wasn't going to be super chatty on the drive to Sowell City.

There wasn't much scenery between the airport and the city, just fields of dust and the occasional trailer, and Baron was the chatty type, at least on long drives, so it wasn't long before he broke and tried again to spark up a conversation. "What brings you to Sowell City? School? Work?"

"I'm just visiting," she said.

"You have a pretty nice pack. Are you a hiker? It's a little late in the season to hike Sowell Gate, but at least the trails shouldn't be too crowded," Baron said.

Genesis nodded, and for the first time since she got in his car, her eyes held a glimmer of amusement. Baron's heart picked up a beat or two as their eyes met, and his eyes were off the road for a bit too long. The loud rattle of his tires hitting the rumble strip had him jerking his head and the wheel back straight.

"You can drop me off once we're in city limits, and I can grab a cab from there. You're probably anxious to get home to your family."

I should be. I really should be.

Her deadpan response after the smoldering look from earlier threw him for a loop. On the one hand, he was excited at the possibility that the attraction he felt wasn't just one-sided. On the other, he may be single, but he wasn't ready to mingle just yet. Then again, if she was, in fact, interested, she probably wasn't looking for something more than just one night.

Baron shook his head. He was projecting. He had no idea what was going through Genesis's mind, and it wasn't his place to guess. He should keep the conversation light to avoid any misunderstandings. Not that he had the slightest chance with the woman sitting next to him. Still, Baron was a talker, and if he couldn't get into what she was doing here in Sowell City, he could at least talk about himself.

Baron kept his eyes on the road but smiled and replied, "I am, but neither my brothers nor my parents are waiting up."

"You live with your parents?" Her eyes widened in disbelief, and Baron couldn't help but laugh. If she was not pleased with that idea, just wait until he shared with her the ultimate red flag.

"Yes, I just got back from finalizing my divorce."

Fool! You are finally interested in a woman after Christine, and you are tanking your chances!

Hell, he shouldn't even be interested, and, to be completely fair, he was grasping at every last crumb that might indicate she was feeling the same pull he was. God, he was such a loser. He just needed to get her safely to her destination without being a creep.

"Oh, I'm sorry."

"Yeah, me too. Anyway, I can take you to your hotel. It's no problem."

"Actually, it is," she said.

"Okay, then I can drop you wherever you feel comfortable."

Baron had only meant to spark up a conversation. Share a bit about himself so she would be more comfortable until they reached her destination. He had not meant to make her more uncomfortable or, worse, feel unsafe with him.

The rest of the drive passed in awkward silence, with Baron occasionally glancing over at the woman. Genesis would look up and catch him looking. Then shake her head before she turned back to look out the window or down at her phone.

He kept his eyes firmly on the road after that. Her body posture had finally relaxed, and he didn't want to risk making her uncomfortable again.

"Is it your first time at Sowell Gate?"

Genesis appreciated his change in conversation. Baron was definitely hot. A little older than the guys she usually went for and definitely full of red flags. Recently divorced, lived with his parents, drove an old beater, and gendered inanimate objects. If he wasn't straight out of the book of Nope, Genesis did not know what kind of guy he was. That was a lie. She had her own chapter of the book of Nope waiting for her back home. She played with the hem of her shirt at the reminder she was only to have a short reprieve from Victor and his misunderstanding of their relationship status. Still, that didn't stop her from being intrigued by Baron. She'd felt his gaze on her at the airport and again in the car, like a trail of liquid fire poured over her skin.

It was a reaction she had felt before. One that under normal circumstances would have her batting her eyelashes and purring naughty things into his ear. The romance novelist in her was all for playing with this dangerous attraction. Even if nothing amounted from it, she could totally use the material for her next Gen Ursa novel. Like she'd done countless times with others in the past. Although, this time was different. She'd never reacted this strongly to anyone so quickly and absolutely never had her Bear also been one hundred percent on board with fucking a stranger. Her Bear had instantly reacted to him, and she'd turned to face the window to avoid him seeing it in her eyes.

That had basically been the entire trip so far. Her finding a level of comfort and then having to turn away before he caught a glimpse of her Bear. It was a testament to how tired she was that she was having such a hard time controlling her shift. A flash of the eyes was one thing. The moment fur sprouted from her brown skin, he'd probably kill them both, losing control of his vehicle.

Talking about hiking allowed her to refocus and regain control. She latched on to that life preserver quick. She'd come to Sowell City—and more specifically, the Sowell Gate area—for answers. Answers about her birth parents that her adopted family hadn't been able to give her.

"I guess I'm like most tourists, interested in Sowell Gate itself," she replied.

Baron chuckled. "Well, there are several trails that will get you some pretty nice pictures of it, but the actual Sowell Gate is restricted land. Not just because it's sacred to the Native people, but because it's dangerous. Don't go up there thinking you can just sneak through. You'll get caught before you can even blink, and or end up dead."

"Thanks for the warning," Genesis said.

"Are you meeting a friend to hike with? It's not a good idea for a woman like yourself to hike alone unless you stick to the beginner trails at the base of the mountain," he said.

Genesis snorted. Maybe she didn't have to be so worried about being attracted to Baron. She traveled and hiked alone all the time. It wasn't that he was wrong about there being added danger for women who traveled alone, but that added danger for women was directly related to the toxic masculinity he was spewing.

"First, I'm not your daughter, old man, don't dad voice me. Second, I can handle myself. This isn't my first solo adventure."

"Old man? Dad voice? I'm not as old as you think. Where am I dropping you?" Baron said.

Genesis checked the time on her phone and sighed. She normally would never give a guy she just met her location plans, but Baron, while totally in the stone age, seemed harmless enough.

"I was hoping to check out Gateway Motel since it's close to the first trailhead," Genesis said.

"What?"

"Gateway Motel," Genesis said.

Baron nearly swerved off the road. His head whipped around so fast. "Oh hell, no! That place is basically condemned and full of unsavory types. I can't in good conscience take you to that shit hole.

Sowell City has plenty of better hotels. Safer hotels. With continental breakfast and free shuttle service to the trails and the airport."

Genesis opened her mouth to put up a fight, but one look at Baron and she shut her mouth. She knew the Gateway Motel wasn't the best. They barely had a website and the reviews—oh god, the reviews—but it was the first place on her list to go hunting for the truth about her past. Genesis fingered the time-worn stationery with the Gateway Motel logo in her pocket.

"I could have just called one of these hotels with a shuttle instead of relying on a strange man to get me into the city." Genesis was pissed that she didn't have a comeback for her choice to stay at an obviously rundown establishment. What she could take issue with was the fact he'd failed to mention any shuttle services when she'd asked about sharing a cab.

Baron's hands gripped the steering wheel a little tighter, and he cursed under his breath before shooting her an apologetic look. "I'm sorry. It slipped my mind, and I assumed maybe you were staying at one of the few hotels that don't offer the service. I couldn't just leave you stranded. My mother raised me better than that."

The softness in his tone when he mentioned his mother had no right to extinguish the burning suspicion that had sprung up inside her, but it did. Baron seemed genuine in his apology too. Before Genesis could process what she was doing, she had reached over and given Baron's massive forearm a squeeze. While he hadn't mentioned an alternative to getting a ride from him, Genesis should have planned this trip better. It was her own impulsiveness and desperation to escape the suffocating cloud of Victor's attention that had her out here unprepared.

"Don't beat yourself up too much. I could have been more prepared myself or simply used the internet to figure that out. Thank you for finally telling me, though. Which of these glorious hotels would you suggest?"

"There's a strip of decent hotels downtown. I can drop you there, and you can choose whichever one. I don't need to know which, like I said. I don't mean to overstep," Baron said.

"Sounds good to me," Genesis replied and reluctantly removed her fingers from his flannel-clad arm.

Her Bear was not happy that Genesis had stopped touching Baron, but a firm reminder that he was human, he couldn't possibly know about Shifters, and she wasn't about to let that cat out of the bag or, more aptly the Bear out of the bag, because of some fleeting attraction, her Bear curled up inside her and pretended to nap. Releasing a relieved sigh, Genesis settled into the seat and turned back to look out the window. It couldn't be long now before they reached the city. Its glittering lights appeared larger on the horizon. All she had to do was wait it out, and she'd never see Baron again.

Genesis pulled out her phone and looked up how much farther to Gateway Motel from the city center, but got distracted by the number of notifications on her screen. She cursed and mentally kicked herself for accidentally hitting send on the photo she took of Baron earlier. She'd had her phone opened to her text thread with Victor.

V: Who the fuck is this?

G: Sorry meant to send that to my cover designer. It's a stock photo.

V: Oh! Where you at now? You didn't give me details about your trip.

G: Just some small town with an awesome mountain range to explore. Anyway, I'm almost out of cell range, so I'll be out of touch for quite a bit.

V: You know I don't like not being able to reach you.

G: I'll call when I'm back. Promise.

When he didn't reply, Genesis let out the breath she'd been holding. She had no intention of calling Victor when she got back. The only thing she planned to do was find a storage unit for her things and continue to travel and write until she felt the need to settle again. With Victor placated, for the time being, she looked up Gateway Motel like she'd originally planned.

Genesis groaned aloud when she saw it was farther out than she'd like. If she couldn't get a cab from the airport, getting one to take her to the rundown motel in the boonies was certainly not going to happen tonight. She'd stay one night at a hotel in the city and then check the place out in the morning before heading out to the mountain.

CHAPTER TWO

Baron was playing with fire. He'd offered the correct reaction to the news of Genesis staying at the rat trap motel when he offered a suggestion of a better place to stay. It was quite a bit better than the urge to demand she share his hotel room. Then again, he wasn't in his right mind, and he knew it. His emotions were all over the place as he processed the finality of his years-long divorce and what that would actually mean for his life. So, he turned the conversation back to her hiking plans, and when they arrived in the downtown area, he tried not to think about the fact that he was dropping her right in front of the hotel he planned to stay in, the Sowell Gate Regency.

Was it a bit shady? Most definitely, but even if he dropped her off right in front of the place, that didn't mean she wouldn't mosey down to another hotel. It didn't mean he'd run into her again before she left for the trails. It was just the possibility that she would choose the same hotel. That maybe he'd run into her at breakfast the next morning and talk her into letting him drive her to the trailhead. Maybe he'd hike the first mile or two with her, just to be sure she wasn't taking on more than she was prepared to handle. Sowell Gate trails were deceptive.

They seemed easy enough, but the weather was unpredictable, and if you strayed from the wide clear path of the well-traveled main trail, there were tons that could go wrong for those unfamiliar with the territory.

"You're frowning. Is something wrong?" Genesis's voice broke into his musings.

He forced a smiled and put his car into park, waving off the valet who immediately recognized him and moved forward to get his keys.

"Nothing you need to worry about. Have a good night, Genesis. I hope you enjoy your time in Sowell City."

She gave him a quizzical look, but then smiled and nodded. "I'm sure I will. Thank you for the lift."

Baron watched as she scrambled out of the car, and at the last second, he had the presence of mind to get out himself to grab her obscenely heavy pack. Once again, the urge to insert himself into her business poked its needy little head, but he shoved the urge down almost as quick. The way she shrugged the pack onto her shoulder as if it weighed nothing told Baron all he needed to know. Genesis could handle her own. Even if he couldn't seem to shake the desperate need to ensure she was okay.

She gave him another smile and a wave, and reluctantly, he got back in the car. He'd park the car himself and then head over to Sowell Garden to grab a bite to eat. Hopefully, that would be enough time for him not to run into Genesis again. Except just as he was about to pull away from the curb, there was a knock on the passenger side window. He looked up to see Genesis signaling for him to roll the window down, so he did.

"Do you know any good restaurants? My first flight was late, and I had to run to get my connection instead of stopping for dinner as I had originally planned," she asked.

The biggest grin Baron had ever grinned spread across his face. "I was just headed to Sowell Garden. Best place in town, if you care to join me."

Genesis was relieved when Baron dropped her off in a very public, very crowded area of downtown Sowell City. That also happened to be right in front of what Genesis could tell was probably the nicest hotel in the small city. At least until he went to pull away, and her Bear started to lose its shit. It raged at her to stop him, to at least get his contact information for future use. It wasn't normal, and it scared her a little, but she was too tired and hungry to fight her Bear for much longer.

So instead of heading into the fancy hotel and treating herself to a comfy hotel stay before roughing it in nature for the next week or so, she found herself tapping on Baron's window just before he pulled away from the curb. The grumble of her stomach gave her the perfect excuse for her odd behavior, and the smile Baron gave her after she asked about a place to eat had eased the Bear's raging, if only by a little.

"So, is this Sowell Garden place any good?"

Baron laughed, "It's the best. Trust me."

Genesis didn't want to trust him. She rarely trusted anyone, but if she had learned anything from the short time she'd known Baron, he somehow had broken through her trust issues. First with his offer of a ride that she'd taken. Second with the fact she hadn't immediately called one of her friends to chat on the drive into town, and again when her Bear inexplicably threw them into the lion's den again by stopping him from leaving.

How long had it been since she'd been set free? Genesis's skin literally itched with the feel of her Bear's fur chaffing just below the surface, reminding her of the reason she'd chosen the Gateway Motel instead of cushier lodgings in town. Not just because it was her only clue to finding her birth parents, but because it was the perfect place for her to stay close to hunter-free woods.

While the idea of staying in a nicer hotel was tempting, she needed a safe place to let her Bear roam. Those tiny bits of freedom were the only thing that kept her sane during the long periods trapped in the confines of her human skin. Finding Baron to be physically attractive was putting them both in danger in ways she couldn't possibly explain to him without sounding like a lunatic. Still, what was becoming very clear to Genesis was that because of her and her Bear's attraction, she wasn't fully in control of herself around Baron.

"I do trust you, but you won't mind if I look the place up while we are on our way there?"

She was taking a risk climbing back into his busted truck and going out to dinner with him.

"It's a short ride, but whatever floats your boat."

According to the internet, Sowell Garden was the must-visit restaurant of Sowell City, second only to its sister establishment, Flower Café. It served Asian fusion, was owned and operated by a respected Korean American family, and the head chef pictured in the short article was labeled as a must-see attraction as well. She snorted at that added tidbit from the blog she'd opened to read about the place.

While there was a decent review of what the restaurant offered and its history, it was very clear the blogger had a huge crush on Chef Kim. Judging by the picture, Genesis could see the man's physical beauty, but he was stiff as a board with crossed arms and a stern scowl on his face, like he was too busy to have been pulled away long enough to take this one picture. Genesis had had dalliances with enough chefs to know the type. Self-important, no time for anything but a quick lay, and you better get yours first.

The opposite of the man sitting beside her who, while confident, held a gentleness to how he carried himself. Like his walls were built after the man and not the other way around. He was friendly and open, but not really open, if that made any sense. The perfect candidate to be converted into one of her brooding male heroes in her novels. Not just in temperament, but in looks as well. He was tall and muscular. He quite literally dwarfed her in size, and that only made her want to climb him like she planned to climb Sowell Gate Mountain. If she wanted to climb him, then so would her readers.

She glanced back at her pack, the urge to whip out her notebook and jot down notes a welcome distraction to her growing attraction for Baron. Only she couldn't reach her pack with the seatbelt on, and Baron was already pulling into a parking space.

"Sowell Garden is usually insanely packed on nights like this. Well, most nights in general, so if you would rather go someplace else," Baron offered.

Genesis snagged her wallet from her pack since they were now parked and shook her head. "Nope, this is fine."

She got out, and Baron scrambled out to meet her before she was fully out of the truck. He took her hand as she hopped down and continued to hold it while he walked the short distance from where he parked to the front of the restaurant. Could she have pulled her hand away? Sure. Did she want to? No. Especially with the calming effect it currently had on her Bear.

Genesis hated that she seemed to need him ever closer to keep her Bear in check. The ride should have been enough. This was too close to feeling like a date. A real date, despite the circumstances that had brought them both there. Especially when, almost as soon as they entered the crowded restaurant, the hostess rushed over with menus in hand.

"Mr. Cross! Your table is already ready," the hostess said.

"You have a table already?" Genesis looked up at Baron, and he shrugged, still not letting go of her hand.

"It's not my table, really. It's the table they keep open for important guests."

"Oh, and you're an important guest?"

"Not me, my family," he replied.

There was nothing about Baron's tone that told Genesis to let the topic drop. It was the sudden tensing of his muscles that she felt in the tightening of his grasp on her hand. The weird part was she didn't even think his family was the issue, but rather, the fact he didn't feel important even if his family obviously had importance enough in town to be automatically recognized and offered a table in a packed restaurant.

The reaction was completely at odds with the confidence Baron basically oozed all over the place. Genesis followed Baron and the hostess to the table anyway, saving any further commentary for when they were seated.

Baron was glad Genesis didn't ask more about his family. It was always easy to forget when he was around new people that not everyone knew about the Cross family. Not everyone knew he bore the weight of being the figurehead of the future of the Cross family legacy. Maybe that was why he hadn't just given her the address to Sowell Garden so she could come here on her own. Why he'd attempted to drop her at the same hotel he'd been staying, but had been too chicken shit to walk in with her.

He liked being judged on his own merits, not on the reputation of his family. Not that he had much merit on his own. Yet, all of that had threatened to catch up to him in his brief reprieve when the hostess had recognized him and ignored his signal to not rush over. He couldn't blame the girl. Most people jumped into action when his family came to the city. They had too much money and too much standing in the community to be seen as indifferent to his status as a Cross.

A status he had handed to him, not one he had earned, and that's what chaffed the most. He hadn't earned anything of worth in his life. His job had been handed to him. He lived on the land earned by his ancestors. Well, earned was being very generous. They'd stolen it plain and simple, and while that was a fact he was well aware of, he still couldn't bring himself to hate or shun the legacy they'd left behind like his younger brothers did.

The hostess left them at the table, and the waitress immediately appeared. "Can I start you off with something to drink, Mr. Cross?"

Baron forced a tight smile at the waitress, who was completely ignoring the fact that Baron still held Genesis's hand in his for all to see on the table. Instead, her eyes were glued to his face, and when he looked up at her, a blush crept into her cheeks. He'd give her a pass, considering she barely looked old enough to legally serve alcohol.

"My date and I would like some time to ponder the menu," he said coolly.

The girl's enamored blush was quickly replaced with an embarrassed one as she finally glanced over at Genesis and then down at their entwined hands and back to him.

"Of course, sir," the waitress said before skittering away. Baron turned his attention back to Genesis, whose head was tilted to the side.

"Your date?" She pulled her hand from his, and the loss of contact felt like a splash of cold water on his face.

Right, this wasn't a date. She wasn't his date. They were two not quite strangers sharing a meal together.

Fuck, what if she's seeing someone?

Baron refused to ask if she was. It wasn't his business, even if he'd like it to be. Genesis didn't seem like she was seeing someone else. She seemed to be sticking to him as much as he wanted to stick to her. She hadn't balked at him holding her hand until his little comment about them being on a date. He was totally overthinking this whole thing and should keep it casual and expectation free.

"Would you rather deal with her fawning over me all evening?"

"I'd rather have ordered so I could get my food faster. The way that girl scampered off to give us time, it will be a miracle if we see her any sooner than 30 minutes before the kitchen closes."

"Do you know what you want already? You haven't even touched the menu," Baron replied.

Genesis smirked. "I knew what I'd order before you even parked the car. The menu is on the internet."

"Oh, but I was so looking forward to giving you my own personal recommendations."

"You strike me as the type who'd order Bulgogi and put ketchup on it," she snorted.

Now Baron was truly offended. "The only thing I've ever put ketchup on after the age of 5 was a hamburger and fries."

Genesis shrugged, "Well then, Mr. Cross. What would you suggest?"

Baron leaned forward, flashing her what he hoped was a charming smile. "Why don't you tell me what you desire to try, and I'll make a recommendation based on that?"

She raised an eyebrow at him and pushed her hair over her shoulder before leaning forward until he felt the heat of her cheek against his own. Her thick lips tickled the side of his ear as she whispered, "What if what I desire isn't on the menu?"

His mouth fell open in shock as Genesis pulled away, a devious grin on her face before she picked up the menu. "Close your mouth, Baron. You'll catch flies."

Genesis held the menu so that it covered her face and hid what was no doubt a horrible grimace as she fought to take control of herself back from her Bear. While Genesis wasn't ashamed of propositioning Baron, she definitely hadn't meant to be so brazen about it before they'd eaten.

What is wrong with you? I thought we had an agreement?

Mine.

Genesis bit her lip hard, the sharp pain directed toward the beast inside her. For years, Genesis had struggled with her other side. First, with understanding what was going on with her. Having been raised a human, she had no concept of Shifters outside of mainstream media. Then later, after finding out the truth about Shifters from a rogue she had encountered on a hiking trip. Her Bear hadn't trusted Mark, but she'd needed his guidance on how the Shifter thing worked. It was then that Genesis and her Bear had struck up a bargain.

As long as Genesis gave the Bear enough outside time in which it was fully in control, she would allow Genesis the peace and control she needed in everyday human interactions. Apparently, her Bear hadn't been given enough outside time. That, and it seemed so outrageously attracted to Baron. The lack of control was concerning and made Genesis want to pull back and put distance between herself and Baron. She took a deep breath and let it out slowly before hazarding a look over the top of the menu. Baron sat on the other side of the table looking at her. He'd closed his mouth, but instead of a passive expression or any lingering shock, his brown eyes were narrowed in her direction, his arms crossed over his broad chest.

The posture reminded her of her high school history teacher, who'd adopt a similar look when the class misbehaved. Her author brain decided to kick in then, filling her mind with images of her in her old school uniform bent over the teacher's desk and getting spanked with a ruler. Only instead of Mr. Matthews, it was Baron doing the punishing. His massive biceps bulging in a white button-down; the sleeves rolled up, of course.

In real life, her eyes met with Baron's over the menu, and the stern, pensive look relaxed, and a spark of curiosity lit his eyes as if he sensed what she was thinking. She opened her mouth in preparation to give some witty retort as the waitress girl returned to their table.

"Um, I'm sorry to bother you, but the kitchen will be closing soon. Have you decided what you would like to eat?"

The girl's interruption was as effective as a bucket of cold water over Genesis's head. Or rather, it should have been. Genesis was slightly miffed at the girl's intrusion, but Genesis's Bear was fucking livid. Genesis gripped the seat of her chair as claws sprang out, piercing the thick wood. She closed her eyes as she could feel them burning gold and didn't want to add to the questions Baron would certainly have about her sudden odd behavior.

Enough! I promise I'll let you out as soon as I can.

Mine!

He'll run if you keep this up!

That seemed to break through the Bear's rage enough for Genesis to retract her claws from the chair and move her hands to her lap, if not back to the menu on the table. She opened her eyes to see Baron giving her a concerned look before he quickly ordered for the both of them.

"We'll both have the sesame honey glazed Mandu to start and the Salmon Bulgogi, medium spice."

"And to drink?" the girl said, completely oblivious to Genesis as she continued to give Baron her undivided attention.

Genesis's Bear continued to press at her skin, but Genesis kept fighting the pull of the shift.

"Water is fine for now, thanks," Baron said.

The waitress nodded and walked away. His quick action and the girl's departure eased her Bear and allowed her back in the driver's seat. Once there, she put as tight a lock as she could on her Bear.

"Thank you," Genesis breathed.

Baron nodded, a glint of amusement in his eyes, "Hunger pains can get the best of us all."

"Was it that obvious?" Genesis smiled, latching onto the easy out he'd provided at her odd behavior.

"Well, it was either that or you really needed to use the restroom," he laughed.

Now that he had mentioned it, Genesis could use a bathroom break. It had been a long drive. "Well, actually. If you'll excuse me?"

She stood, and Baron, ever the gentleman, stood too. She glanced over her shoulder to find him watching her as she scurried to the restroom. After relieving herself, Genesis took a moment to splash some water on her face and have a chat with her Bear.

What the fuck was that?

We want him.

Ugh! Of all times for you to be on board with hooking up, why now? Why him?

You know why!

I obviously don't, and I definitely don't appreciate what happened back there. You better cut the crap, or I'll make sure to end things right after dinner.

You wouldn't!

I most certainly would. Don't try me again.

When her Bear didn't respond, Genesis took a deep breath and released it, shaking out her shoulders to release the tension that had built there. As interesting as Baron was, that didn't mean she'd had plans on hopping into bed with him. She was on this trip to climb mountains, not emotionally unavailable men. Then again, who said emotions had to be involved? She'd surely fucked people without them before. What would make Baron any different? Genesis would see how dinner went. If she was stuck in the city for another night, maybe blowing off some steam with her hot new acquaintance was just what she needed. She touched up her lip gloss and squared her shoulders before heading back to the table.

Baron hid a smirk behind his napkin as he wiped his mouth. He was done with his food, but Genesis was currently savoring every bit of the lychee sorbet he'd ordered for dessert. He couldn't feel even the tiniest bit of upset that she'd commandeered his dessert after stating how full she was from the main course. The pure bliss on her face and the tiny moans of pleasure as she scooped more of the translucent confection into her mouth had all sorts of naughty fantasies running through his brain.

"I take it you like my choice in dessert?"

She paused in the middle of licking the last bit of sorbet from the tiny dessert spoon and nodded enthusiastically. "Oh, I most certainly do. It was sweet, tangy, but light and refreshing. I could totally see describing female arousal with this flavor profile. I bet my hero would overcome his phobia of orally pleasing his mate if she tasted this scrumptious."

Almost as soon as she finished her sentence, she froze, and her eyes widened in shock. Probably matching Baron's own shock at her words. Despite their earlier conversation, Baron had no idea if Genesis was actually single or not. Now hearing that her supposed hero wasn't pulling his weight in the pleasure department had him spitting mad and eager to show her what a real man could offer her.

"Well, I'd say any man who's afraid to please his woman in any fashion isn't much of a man at all, but having tasted Chef Kim's lychee sorbet, I can say if a woman tasted as satisfying and complex on my tongue, I'd never come up for air."

Genesis cleared her throat before breaking eye contact with him. "Is that so?"

He reached over and drew her gaze back to his. He trailed his finger along her jaw before letting it fall back to the table. "If I'm being completely honest, I'm a little rusty in the intimacy department given my current relationship status, but when I'm ready to put myself out there, God help the woman who lands in my bed."

That seemed to break the tension between them as Genesis laughed so long and hard that Baron was suddenly self-conscious about his self-deprecating brag.

"God help her, indeed. If you put in work half as good as your charm, I might be tempted to give you my number. You know, for when you're ready?"

"You planning to be in town for a while?"

"No, but my bed is open tonight." Genesis couldn't believe she'd just said that out loud.

Baron sat back in shock, and she slapped a hand over her mouth. There was an awkward moment where they just stared at each other. The embarrassment she felt shifted as she registered the shock in his eyes was fading into something else. However, before he could speak, an Asian man in a chef's coat came up to the table.

"Mr. Cross, thank you so much for dining with us this evening. I hope everything was to your liking?"

When Baron didn't immediately answer, the man's gaze traveled to Genesis, and she nearly choked on her own tongue as she realized it was Chef Kim. The freaking Chef Kim. The internet had not lied about his looks, but she was currently too mortified to even speak. Baron recovered quicker than she did.

"Yes, everything was fantastic as always. My friend was just swooning over your lychee sorbet."

The chef raised an eyebrow at Baron calling me his friend but didn't comment. Instead, he smiled and nodded.

"Ah well, would you like another order? I see the one you two were sharing is finished."

Baron looked at her, and she shook her head, so he responded for both of them. "That would be lovely, but can we take it to-go? It's getting late, and I'd like to get her back to her hotel."

"Of course," Chef Kim replied and walked off while Genesis glared at Baron.

"Oh my god! He's going to think we're going to do naughty things with his food," she gasped.

Baron laughed, "Are we not?"

Genesis shook her head. "Don't you need to get home?"

"I made hotel reservations for the night. It's a bit longer of a drive home than I'm prepared for right now."

"Oh, well..." Genesis said.

He reached across the table and took her hand in his. "Nothing has to happen between us. Not tonight or ever, but I would like to at least make sure you get to your hotel okay. And if you'd like to share more of my dessert, that's fine. We can stop there if that's what you want."

NO! We want more! Tell him we want more!

Hush!

"I'll think about it," Genesis said instead.

She really did need to think about it. Unlike Baron, she didn't currently have a reservation at any hotel. Although the one he had dropped her off in front of seemed nice enough.

"Okay, have you decided on which hotel you are staying in?"

"Uh, maybe the one you dropped me off at? It looked nice."

"It is nice, and I happen to be staying there as well."

"Is that right?" Genesis laughed. Of course, that was where he was staying.

It's fate.

It's a setup.

We agreed.

I know.

Just then, the waitress approached with the bill and the to-go container for the lychee sorbet. Genesis reached for the bill, but Baron grabbed it first and stuffed a couple of bills inside.

"My treat," Baron said, handing the bill back to the waitress.

"I can pay for myself," Genesis insisted once the waitress left.

"You can pay next time," Baron said and stood from the table. He was already walking away before she could protest, and she was forced to follow after him.

Baron sighed with relief, even though his shoulders were tense as fuck. He had no business pursuing this attraction he had for Genesis, but for some reason, despite his better judgment, he continued to push. Not just his boundaries but hers.

"There might not be a next time," Genesis muttered as he helped her into his truck.

He smirked and shut the door before rounding the truck and climbing in next to her.

"Let's hurry back. I don't want our dessert to melt before we can thoroughly enjoy it."

Only by the time they reached the hotel, Genesis was nodding off, and while Baron was horny as fuck, he wasn't asshole enough to push for them to end the night together in his bed. The lobby of the Sowell Gate Regency was dead this time of night. Most of the people had already retired to their rooms, and the bartender in the lounge was wiping things down while the hostess encouraged the late-nighters to retire to their rooms as well.

"You look dead on your feet. Let me handle the reservations, and we'll get you in bed in no time."

"Really? No time?"

"I mean, if that isn't what you want..."

"I'm exhausted for sure, but..."

"No buts, it's settled. Let's get you a room."

"Mr. Cross, we have your room ready for you. Are you sure you wouldn't like to upgrade?" the receptionist asked when he approached the front desk.

"An upgrade won't be necessary, but I would like to add a room to my reservation for my friend."

Genesis glared at him, but he ignored it as the receptionist did as he asked. She didn't say anything when the receptionist gave him the total for their one-night stay. He wasn't certain of Genesis's financial situation, but the price tag was one even he itched to reject, but it was his own machinations that brought them here, so he should be the one to foot the bill.

"You didn't have to pay for my room. It's bad enough you paid for dinner," Genesis said as they rode the elevator up together.

"I didn't have to pay for your room, but I wanted to. Don't think too much about it. Anyway, it was nice to meet you, Genesis. I hope you have a nice time up on the mountain," he said.

"Thank you," Genesis replied.

Her room was next to his, an adjoining room, and Baron willed himself not to press the issue. He opened the door, fully prepared to go into his room alone. At the last second, Genesis placed her hand on his arm.

"I know it's late, but I'm not quite ready to retire. Let me buy you a drink at the bar?"

"Sure, we can have a drink, but let's hit up the minibar instead. Shower, get comfortable, and join me?" he suggested.

He was taking a risk by inviting her into his room. Despite their flirtations, things were still rocky if they were both willing and able to act upon them. Even if she accepted his offer, he wouldn't push, at least not tonight.

"That's not the same," Genesis said.

"But that's the deal, take it or leave it."

"Fine," she said and let go of his arm.

"Any preference on the choice of beverage? I can always call down to order something specific if they haven't stocked what you prefer."

"Any kind of beer is fine," she said before disappearing into her room.

Baron smirked and let himself into his room. After shoving the already melting sorbet into the tiny freezer, he checked the mini bar. It had an assortment of liquor but no beer, so he called down to the front desk. He ordered a couple of beers before opening the door between their two rooms for Genesis and heading to wash the grime of the day off his body. The hotel shower was too small for him, but he did the best he could to maneuver and reach all of his body.

The warm water relaxed his muscles and the weight of the day felt even heavier on his shoulders. He was free of Christine, but he still felt trapped, like she still had her sharp talons in his back. He snatched the towel off the rack before wrapping it around his waist and storming out of the bathroom. He froze when he saw Genesis perched on the edge of his hotel bed. Dressed in a pair of shorts and a tank top; one of those with a little scrap of fabric to act as a bra of sorts, but did nothing to hide the way her nipples budded at the sight of him in a towel.

She bit her lip and stood.

"Uh, beer is already here. I'll give you some space to... uh... get dressed, and just knock when you are decent," she rambled and made a move for the door.

Baron caught her arm before his brain caught up to his body's movements. He released her and shook his head. "Sorry, I... I'll change in the bathroom," he muttered.

Get a fucking grip, man.

Baron was out of his depth here. He was acting out of character, or at least out of character for the man he thought he'd grown into. He wasn't some overzealous teenage boy or an arrogant early twenty-something. He was a grown-ass man, and he needed to act like it. He hadn't realized he'd still been standing there with just the tiny towel barely holding together across his broad hips until Genesis took a seat on the edge of the bed farthest from him.

Baron sighed with relief that she hadn't immediately run for the hills with his brutish behavior. Still, he needed to put some damn clothes on before he felt she would be comfortable, so he reached for his suitcase. Which was already open on the floor. Unfortunately, the towel that barely shielded his manhood came undone at the slightest bit of pressure. It fell to the floor, and he cursed just as he heard Genesis's soft gasp.

He glanced up, his fingers hovering above the dropped towel, and caught her staring. Not hiding her eyes or the lust in them as she took in his naked form.

"I'm sorry," he said, quickly tearing his gaze away and snatching up the towel.

He had just barely righted himself with the towel in front of him when she stood abruptly and crossed the distance between them.

"You don't play fair," Genesis said.

"I don't play anything. I'll just hop into the bathroom to finish changing, and then we can hang out," Baron said and practically fled into the tiny bathroom.

The atrociously minuscule towel did nothing to hide his state of arousal, and after sliding on his boxers, he closed his eyes and did his best to put a lid on his inappropriate thoughts about Genesis.

"Are you alright in there? I can leave if that would make you more comfortable," Genesis's voice called through the door.

A slice of panic shot through him. He didn't want her to leave. He just needed a moment to cool off. To remember that he was, in fact, a gentleman in charge of his own body. He slid on his pajama pants next before nearly ripping the door off its hinges as he barreled out of the tiny claustrophobic space.

"Uh, sorry to keep you waiting," he said sheepishly before joining her on the bed. He sat on the opposite corner as her, and she passed him the second beer from the room service tray.

"Waiting for your presence or waiting for you to make a move on me?"

Baron shook his head. "I'm not going to lie and say I don't want you, Genesis. You're sexy as hell, and we're also grown-ass adults who can handle a no-strings-attached romp if that was on the table. However, you've made it clear that isn't what you want, and I am okay with that. Even if it means after this beer, we respectfully part ways, and I spend the night desperately horny and alone," he said.

"Desperately horny, huh?"

"I haven't been with a woman in over three years. Haven't really wanted to until today, so yeah, desperately horny is the correct phrasing," he said.

Genesis choked on her beer so bad that Baron moved closer to pat her back to make sure she didn't die on him.

"Three! Three years? Seriously?"

Baron shook his head. "I'm a loyal man. I couldn't take another woman while still married, and hell, to be honest, me and my wife hadn't been intimate for a while, even before that. I'm not saying this to guilt you into sleeping with me. I'm just being honest."

Genesis knew he wasn't trying to guilt her into sleeping with him, and he wasn't. Fuck, this man was something else. *If* she overlooked his red flags, he was loyal, caring, sexy, and had a monster cock. No, she didn't feel spurred on by guilt, but instead by her own fucked up psychosis of wanting a taste of a man she had no business being with.

After her gasping subsided, he scooted back to his corner of the bed, and she missed the warmth of him behind her. It was then she made her final decision. Baron was definitely going to get it tonight. Her Bear wholeheartedly agreed and pushed itself forward. Genesis hadn't expected her Bear to be so eager to be involved. It had never done so before. Always allowing Genesis full control in intimate situations. Then again, her Bear had been acting out of sorts ever since they'd laid eyes on Baron at the airport.

Genesis launched herself at him. Climbing onto his lap, she pressed her mouth to his. He tensed for a second before his body relaxed and his lips opened for her. Genesis rubbed herself on his lap, and he wrapped an arm around her waist to hold her steady right on the rigid length of him.

"Genesis, Genesis, love, slow down," he gasped between kisses.

"Not a chance," she replied, slipping her hands between them to free his massive cock.

Baron groaned as she fisted him with both hands, letting her body slide down his until she was kneeling between his thick muscular thighs. She flicked her gaze up, watching the heat in his eyes flare into an inferno when she took the head of him in her mouth.

Genesis knew her limits, this was as far as she could go with her mouth, but it seemed to be enough.

His initial protests died, replaced with a lot of "oh shits" and "fucks" as she worked him. His massive palms cradled her head, gently guiding her further and further down his cock. She allowed it for a few seconds before she pulled away entirely.

"Genesis," he breathed, reaching for her, but she shook her head before pulling her tank top off and shimmying out of her shorts.

"You strike me as a guy who is used to being in control. The kind of guy who likes to set the pace and drive the action. I'm telling you now, that's not how I work."

Baron had the nerve to smirk. "And how do you work?"

Genesis moved a few steps away from the bed, willing her Bear to take a backseat for a moment while she gave them both time to think about what would happen next. As it was, she felt bad for pushing him when he'd asked her to slow down. "If you aren't okay with continuing this or anything else while we are together, tell me."

Baron's eyes darkened, and she expected him to tell her he wasn't okay, but instead, he smirked, "My safe word is red. What's your safe word?"

Genesis couldn't help but grin at the fact that he was asking her about her safe word. Maybe he wasn't as inexperienced as she previously thought? "My safe word is stop."

"Noted," Baron said before lunging forward.

Genesis was too quick for him; she dodged his advance. Then used his momentum to get him on his hands and knees. She straddled him before landing a solid smack across his taut ass. His back arched, his spine pressing against her clit.

Genesis rocked her hips, sliding up and down his back, getting herself off on the subtle ridge of his spine, and fuck, she didn't care how weird it was, and apparently, Baron didn't either. She could feel his labored breathing, smell his arousal mixing with hers.

"Fuck, if you come on my back instead of my dick, I'm going to be pissed," he snarled.

Genesis giggled and rubbed herself harder against him, crying out as she did exactly what he had warned her against. She rode his back to the very end, spreading her juices all over him. Then she moved off him and sat on the edge of the bed, tugging him until his face was right at her dripping wet pussy.

"Clean me up like a good boy, and then I'll allow you to have me," she said.

Baron glared at her before diving right in. All the play in her was forgotten after the first broad stroke of his tongue, and Baron was clearly aware of that fact because before she knew it, he was lifting her body off the bed, or maybe she was floating. She couldn't tell. Not with the wild waves of her second orgasm upon her.

"Baron!" she cried. Her voice harsh and growly, part Genesis, part Bear.

She was losing control, spiraling on his wicked tongue until he let up, allowing her to drift from Cloud Nine back down to Cloud Seven or Eight. Baron repositioned their bodies so he could watch her as he fumbled with the condom. In all his efforts, he never tore his gaze away from her body, his face an intense combination of lust and concentration as he studied her naked form. She could feel the heat of his gaze as it traveled over her taut nipples and down to the apex of her legs, then back up to her face.

"Fucking beautiful," he murmured as he slid on a condom.

He pressed her legs wide and positioned his sheathed dick right at her core. "I was going to be gentle with you, but after the stunt you just pulled, you're lucky I only got two condoms. This first one is going in this naughty little pussy of yours, and the second, well, we'll get to that later," he said before penetrating her.

Genesis dug her heels into the mattress in a failed attempt to get leverage during his ruthless pounding, but she lost all ground as the third and then the fourth orgasm coursed through her. She was so lost in the pleasure, but she had to keep some of her wits about her; otherwise, her Bear was going to make an unwanted appearance. As it was, the Bear was itching to come to the surface, thrashing at her insides, ready to take this male as her own.

"Fuck, fuck! No!" Genesis cried.

Baron stilled above her before pulling all the way out and off the bed.

"Was that a 'no, why does this feel so amazing' or a 'no, get the fuck off me'?" he asked, staring her dead in the eyes.

Genesis closed her eyes, fighting her Bear and taking deep breaths until her Bear finally subsided.

"That no was more of a how the fuck am I coming a fourth time, and you're still hard? Not a stop, definitely not a stop," she said.

Baron looked her over before crawling back onto the bed. His whole demeanor was different. No longer the amped-up sex machine, but a gentle giant as he pressed soft kisses up her abdomen to her mouth. He sipped so sweetly at her lips as he guided her arms around his neck. When he entered her this time, it was slow and gentle. Instead of brute force, he took long, measured strokes that left a trail of sparks along her nerve endings.

This time when she came, it wasn't some instant mass explosion but a slow build-up to a Fourth of July finale of internal fireworks. Baron kept his steady rhythm even as she clawed up his back and dug her heels into his hips.

"Baron, Baron, oh!" She trembled beneath him, the flood unleashing a torrent of emotion she'd never experienced before, and the smell of their sex was suddenly overpowered by something else entirely; her scent mark. It wasn't the fact that it happened. It was the intensity of it that shocked her. It had never come out this sweet or pungent before, like cherries and almonds.

She froze, but Baron didn't seem to notice as he too stilled above her, his thick cock pulsing inside of her as he spilled into the condom. He showered her with kisses until the heat of their activities faded from their bodies.

"Get some rest before I'm ready for you again, Genesis," Baron mumbled against her neck before he started snoring. Not super loud, but definitely there, a low rumble that lulled her to sleep as well.

Baron jerked awake as the sunlight hit his face the next morning. He had always been an early riser, his internal clock waking him well before the first rays peeked over the horizon. Yet, the sun was high in the sky now. He ran a hand over his face and sat up in bed. A soft mewling sound was the first thing that alerted him he wasn't alone.

He looked down to find Genesis, the young woman who'd utterly destroyed him last night. He hazarded a glance at the second condom still unopened on the nightstand. She was splayed naked on the bed, her dark nipples looking like chocolate drops ready to be savored, but he kept his hands to himself. Tearing his gaze away from her exposed bosom, he reached over the condom to the hotel phone and ordered breakfast for them before heading to the bathroom.

He was slightly faster at showering this time, now that he knew just how to position himself to get the best coverage in the tiny stall. He noticed her smell clung to his skin, even after scrubbing down with the hotel's overly perfumed soap. He smiled, not minding the reminder of her, convinced that when she eventually woke up, she'd kick his ass to the curb.

He paused. She wasn't kicking him to the curb. They'd agreed to a no-strings night of fun, and that was it. Baron splashed some cold water on his face as if that would help rid himself of the attachment he could already sense forming between him and Genesis. He needed to get a grip. A knock on the hotel room door tore him out of his depressing thoughts long enough to trade out the old room service tray for the new one. Genesis had shifted position, giving him a good look at the large brown globes of her ass, but was still sound asleep. He laid out their breakfast before climbing onto the bed. He touched her shoulder lightly.

"Genesis," he said.

She didn't move.

He shook her gently. "Genesis, time to wake up," He tried again.

This time she muttered something unintelligible and pulled the blankets over her head. He sighed and got up from the bed, turning to grab all the bedding behind him and snatch it away from her body.

"What the fuck?" she growled, sitting straight up.

Her hair, which had been neatly plated on the sides of her head, was now frizzy and half undone. Her eyes weren't even open as she scowled at the wall instead of at him.

"Breakfast," Baron said.

Genesis's eyes flew open, and she frantically searched for something to cover her body, so he tossed her discarded pajamas.

"Thank you," she muttered before slipping them on.

She looked like she was about to go back to sleep but instead, she crawled across the bed and pulled him down to kiss her.

"Guess you're not worried about morning breath," he teased.

Her response was to nip his lip and drag him back into bed with her. As much as Baron would have loved to get back inside of her, he knew it was a bad idea. Not only because it was way later than he expected, but also because he'd apparently forgotten how to fuck without a lingering attachment.

Genesis pouted when he pulled away from her. "Seriously? When you said one night, I didn't think you would be so literal about it," she grumbled.

"Me either, but it's getting late, and I've got to get back home," he said.

"Right." Genesis nodded slowly before climbing off the bed and heading to her unused room.

"Where are you going? I got us breakfast."

She paused before snatching one of the pancakes off a plate and shoving the whole thing into her mouth and downing it with the orange juice. "Thanks for breakfast and the lay, but I don't want to hold you up," she said.

Baron knew she wasn't saying that in a snotty kind of way, but it still rubbed him all the way wrong. "Holding me up wasn't a problem last night," he snapped.

She stared at him for a moment before rolling her eyes. "I'm beginning to see why your wife divorced your ass," she shot back before storming into the other room.

He followed her. "You have no fucking idea what you're talking about. I divorced her, not the other way around," he said.

She dropped her clothes on the bed and headed into the bathroom as if he wasn't right behind her the whole time. "Again, none of my business," she said, turning on the water.

She stepped inside after slipping on the plastic shower cap provided by the hotel. Baron may be pissed, but the sight of the water sluicing over her bountiful brown curves had him wishing he was the one sliding all over her. He followed the trail as it washed over her shoulders and down her back, tumbling over the gentle folds around her midsection before combining to trickle between her ass cheeks.

"Are you just going to stand there and watch?" she asked, shooting him a teasing grin over her shoulder.

Baron would have given anything to join her under the spray, but if it was even possible, her shower was even smaller than the one in his hotel room. Even if he could squeeze himself in there with her, neither would have space to maneuver in the way he would need to deliver the kind of pleasure she deserved. However, that didn't mean he couldn't help her in other ways.

Baron snatched the washrag from her hands and used it as a physical shield from his arousal as he ran it along her body. She shifted slightly as he washed her inner thigh, his thumb catching her bare folds, and he dropped the towel and the act. He pressed two thick fingers inside of her, and she immediately began to move her hips, riding his hand as the hot water splashed over her body and all over the bathroom floor. Neither of them cared. She didn't take long to come, her juices filling his palm with its sticky sweetness before he lifted her out of the shower.

"I have exactly one condom and one hour," he grumbled as he carried her back to his room.

"I guess you'll have to eat during that time as well," she giggled, and Baron raised an eyebrow at her, suddenly getting an idea.

He'd never actually done food play before, but Genesis had a way of breaking all the preconceived notions and previously hard-set rules he'd ever set for himself when it came to matters of the bedroom. He set her down on the bed and grabbed the food tray and his last condom.

"I am a big fan of multitasking," he said.

CHAPTER THREE

Genesis watched Baron's beat-up old truck drive away from the trailhead with a big grin on her face. Even if the rest of her trip was a bust, at least it had started in a memorable way. She double-checked her backpack before hefting it onto her shoulders.

She had meant to start this hike way earlier in the day, but she wasn't too far off her schedule that she couldn't still make her first campsite in time to set up before sundown. Once there, she would text Baron that she had made it along with the coordinates. He was such a worrier, not liking at all that she not only planned to hike Sowell Gate Mountains on her own but that she actually planned to camp overnight to maximize her time on the mountain. When he realized he couldn't change her mind, he made her promise to send him these updates for the remainder of her trip as an emergency precaution.

To be honest, Genesis was touched by his concern. It was rare that anyone gave a shit about her other than her adoptive parents, and even they had never cared that she liked to hike strange mountains alone for weeks on end. They just thought it was a quirk, not a necessity like it actually was. That was the problem when a Shifter child was raised by humans. They were in grave danger of injuring others, and themselves, trying to figure their shit out. Genesis had always known she was different, and thankfully her first shift at sixteen had been on a camping trip like this one. If it weren't for the Wolf Shifter who'd found her and mentored her that first year, Genesis would have been lost. It was only then that she began to research what happened to her real parents.

She had never expected the tale she eventually uncovered.

A pair of college kids had found her in the woods on one of their own hiking trips wrapped in a fur blanket, a note rolled up around the key chain for the Gateway Motel. All the note had said was that Genesis's mother had been on the run from her abusive father and to take care of her and keep her away from Sowell City at all costs. That obviously hadn't happened; otherwise, Genesis wouldn't be there.

Her mentor had warned her against coming as well, but even he hadn't been able to stop her. So here she was, hiking the exact mountain her birth mother had taken great efforts to keep her away from and hating how much it felt like home. If it weren't for her gear, Genesis would have already shifted to her Bear form, but she wanted to make camp first. The closer she got to her stopping point, the further she felt like going. She caught glimpses of Sowell Gate over the trees as she hiked, and it was gorgeous, so beautiful, and it had this magnetism about it. She could feel its energy even from here, beckoning her closer like a siren's call. The only thing that stopped her from pushing past her first camp was the way her Bear pushed at her skin to be set free.

Her Bear needed her freedom too, so Genesis shot Baron a quick text with her coordinates and made quick work of setting up the bare minimum she needed to be comfortable later that night. Then she shed her clothes and set her Bear free. Sowell Gate Mountains were beautiful in human form, but in her Bear form, they literally came alive. Genesis let her human mind rest so her Bear could handle the reigns for a bit. She could admit she was tired, but the Bear wasn't. She trusted her enough not to take advantage of her freedom while she took a short mental nap.

Home!

I'd always known where we were meant to be. I just couldn't push my human too far too soon. But now we were here and with our mate! I had to find a way to make her stay. The cool mountain air was filled with a symphony of smells, some animal, some not. The leaves rustled overhead, the soft decaying foliage beneath my paws. It was heaven. I was home, and so was Genesis.

I pushed myself farther and faster, following the energetic pull of the mountain, higher and higher. We needed more of this. Time away from the stench of the city. So claustrophobic with its rough concrete and tall buildings that blocked the glorious sun. Not to mention the one she'd left behind. The bad man. His energy was dark, and I was glad to be leaving him behind. Even if only for a short while.

Baron tried to play it cool as he checked his phone, but the grin that spread across his face at the picture Genesis sent, along with her coordinates, was a dead giveaway.

"Your hitchhiker send you a naughty photo?" Hunter teased.

They were in the den sipping whiskey and playing their weekly poker game. Baron set down his phone and scowled at his cousin. "She isn't a hitchhiker. I gave her a ride as a Good Samaritan."

Hunter nudged Baron's younger brother Braxton with a wink.

"He gave her a ride, alright. This dirty fucker couldn't even be bothered to wash away her perfume before coming home," Braxton snickered.

"You're one to talk. How long did you try to hide your relationship with Carmen from us?" he replied.

Now if ever there was a fated love story it would be Braxton and Carmen. Braxton went from swearing he would never be tied down at Bechet and Isis's high society wedding, to only a week later chasing after Carmen like his life depended on it. Baron was a little iffy on the details because he'd been too engrossed in getting rid of Christine, but from what Hunter had whispered in his ear, there had been enough will they or won't they angst to rival any one of those daytime soap operas.

Braxton scowled at him. "I didn't hide anything. Things were complicated."

"Yeah, so complicated you had to trap her ass with a baby, even after she already agreed to marry you," Hunter said.

"Keep talking, like you weren't being strung on by the Falconer Twins," Braxton spat back.

"Firstly, they aren't twins, and second, fuck you, Brax. No offense to Carmen and Isis, but fuck if I let a woman run me, the way y'all let these women run you," Hunter said.

Bechet and Braxton may have gotten their fairy tale romance but Hunter was living up his fuckboy status with zero remorse. Well, he had been until whatever went down that got him tangled up with the Falconers. The fact that he was even associating with anyone from Sullah was a miracle in itself. Let alone any romantic entanglement. The whole thing had star crossed love written all over it. Hunter was still young and full of reckless energy, so only time would tell if he would ever mature enough for a real relationship. In the meantime, Baron, Braxton, and Bechet would enjoy taking full advantage of using the messy situation with the Falconers against their beloved younger cousin.

Baron and Braxton exchanged looks over their sips of whiskey, trying to decide who was going to say it first. Baron set his glass down and smirked at Hunter.

"Like what the Falconers are doing with you is any different," Baron said.

Hunter stood so quick to get in Braxton's face that his chair toppled over. "What the fuck you just say?"

Baron sat back as Braxton just shrugged and took a casual sip of whiskey. "You heard me correctly," Braxton said.

Baron wasn't the kind of man who paid mind to gossip, but seeing his favorite cousin so out of sorts was the perfect escape from the battle he was waging against his building attachment to Genesis. Even though he'd been vaguely aware of Hunter's ill-fated encounter with the Falconer siblings, he had been too focused on his own drama to know all the details.

"Oh, a love triangle. Tell me more," Baron chuckled. Both men turned on him. They knew gossip wasn't his thing, but at least Braxton seemed to get that he was just messing around to get under Hunter's skin.

"According to Carmen, Vega has the hots for one of her brother's friends, but she was using Hunter to make him jealous enough to act on the attraction," Braxton supplied.

Baron scowled at Hunter. "Why the fuck would you go along with that?"

"Because Hunter and Vega's brother had a bad romance. Anyway, Vega dumped Hunter's ass a long time ago, but he's still hung up on the pair of them for some reason," Braxton filled in.

Baron shook his head and downed the rest of his drink. "That's messed up, even for you, Hunter. Fucking a brother and sister? Is there any line you won't cross?"

"I don't gotta listen to this nonsense. Y'all two finish without me," Hunter said and stormed out of the den.

As soon as Hunter was gone, Braxton filled Baron's glass with more whiskey. "So you wanna talk about it?"

"Talk about what?" Baron replied.

Braxton shrugged. "I don't know, your divorce being final? The rebound fling that's obviously not just a fling to you?"

Baron snatched up his glass and downed the entire contents in one gulp. "Fuck no! How's my nephew doing? He sleeping through the night yet?"

Braxton's face lit in the way only a new father's would to talk about his child and started extolling Baron with all the virtues of his three-month-old. Baron had thought his brother's son would bring back too many bad emotions for him, but the opposite had happened. Baron found he wasn't less interested in his new nephew after his divorce but more so. Having a baby around the estate had brought new life to the place.

They chatted about diapers and baby-proofing the cabin for a while before talk turned to prepping the estate for the winter. The year before last, the snow had hit early, and they had been grossly unprepared. If the storm had lasted a day or two longer, they all would have been at each other's throats. Last year hadn't been much better, but the snow had come right on schedule, so they'd had time to prepare. This year, however, he and his brothers weren't taking any chances and had started the winter prep weeks ago.

Come to think of it, that crazy blizzard had hit around this time. His gut tightened at the thought, and Baron shivered. Not with the reminder of the stressful family togetherness but at the thought of Genesis being caught on the mountain in a freak storm such as that one. He pulled out his phone and texted her.

B: Hey! Any chance you have a sat phone or emergency radio?

He waited for her reply. Her campsite was still within range of the cell towers, and she had already set up camp, as shown in her pictures. She should have replied fairly quickly, but as minutes turned into an hour with no contact, Baron cursed and stood.

"Hey, uh, I gotta make a quick run," he said to Braxton before heading straight to the emergency supplies closet. He grabbed two radios, a headlamp, and the keys to the trail runner.

Genesis woke to her Bear so deep in the woods she wasn't even sure how far she'd gone. She pushed herself to the forefront and made her Bear take her back to the campsite.

That's the last time I let you drive if you insist on pushing my boundaries.

Her Bear just chuffed and ignored her. They didn't have that kind of relationship, and Genesis knew that. Soon, they were back in somewhat familiar territory, but something was off. She could sense that someone was at her camp.

"Genesis!"

She cursed and forced herself to shift back to human form. Luckily, her tent had two entrances, and she was able to sneak inside and slip on a shirt before emerging like she'd been asleep.

"Dude, what the hell, Baron?"

He glared at her wide-eyed before pulling her into his arms. "I just checked your tent. You weren't in it," he said.

"I dig a little into the ground in case unwanted visitors come. It looks like my camp is empty," she lied, but now that she thought of it, it wasn't actually a bad idea.

"Oh, well, that's smart. Fuck, I'm sorry. I texted you, and you didn't reply, so I got worried something had happened."

Genesis kissed him to cut off his rambling. "Anyone ever tell you that you worry too much?" She laughed.

Baron laughed too and nodded. "Yeah, they have, but usually those same people come to appreciate it."

"Thank you for coming to check on me, but I'm fine. I was just sleeping," she said.

"Okay, well. I didn't mean to interrupt your sleep. I just brought you this. I know you have a phone, but the next leg of your planned hike will put you out of range of the cell towers. I didn't want you up here stranded with no way of letting someone know if there was a problem," Baron said, pulling a radio out of his pocket.

"Someone like the authorities, or someone like you, Baron?" Genesis asked.

Even though he'd used one hand to bring out the radio, his other was firmly on her bare ass. "Definitely me if you're sleeping out here with nothing but a fucking shirt on," he growled.

Genesis licked her lips. "Well, if that's all," she said and started to turn away, but he held her firmly against his body before reaching into the off-roader she had just registered was there and producing a slim red bag with *emergency kit* written in reflective letters.

"Preset one on the radio is to reach me. Preset two is the park service. I brought you this as well. It has a thermal blanket and slim emergency flares. A couple other things. One can never be too prepared," he said.

Genesis reached between them to grab the bulge in his jeans. "Tell me, Captain Over-prepared. How many condoms are in this surprise emergency kit you brought me?"

Baron hissed as she gave him an extra firm squeeze.

"None," he said.

"Oh," she said and took a step back, but then he picked her up and carried her back into her tent.

"They're all in my back pocket," he said, pulling out a strip of at least seven.

"Okay, I officially appreciate your worrying," Genesis laughed before stripping off her t-shirt.

Baron hadn't planned on spending the night with Genesis at her camp, but he'd be a liar if he claimed he hadn't planned to at least fuck her a few times before he left. Unfortunately, he underestimated both his ability to control himself with her and the amount of energy she literally drained his ass of with her special brand of lovemaking.

Aside from many more condoms to dispose of, the only difference between their first night and this one was that Genesis woke before him, and she definitely did not have the same hang-ups about touching him while he slept. He woke up to her thick lips slurping on his morning wood, and man, was it a pretty fucking sight first thing in the morning.

He tried to pull her up to finish in her pussy, but she fought him off, making him shoot all over her face and breasts.

"Shit, Genesis. I'm sorry."

"Don't be," she laughed, cleaning herself with a wet wipe.

They made out for a few minutes before getting dressed. He reminded her which frequency to use to reach him and the ranger station before forcing himself back onto the trail runner and heading home. Genesis had offered to make him breakfast, but he'd used the excuse of not wanting to use up all of her supplies to get the hell out of dodge before he did anything more reckless, like catch feelings he couldn't shake after a few months.

Baron managed to make it back to the main house on Cross estate without anyone the wiser, but as soon as he stepped out of the garage where the trail runner was kept, he found Hunter leaning against the sidewall.

"Boy, you are one pussy-whipped motherfucker," Hunter said, shaking his head.

Baron frowned at his cousin. Hunter was an asshole by default. He typically wasn't one to lash out without provocation. Then again, Baron had made the rude comment about Hunter's sexuality, and while Hunter knew Baron didn't care about all that, he couldn't be certain it hadn't been taken as the joke he'd meant it to be. Either way, Hunter's attitude wasn't appreciated, and with the smell of alcohol wafting off him, now wasn't the time to try to broach any serious topics.

"I'm gonna let that slide 'cause it's early, and I can smell the whiskey on you still. Go sleep it off before you say or do anything else you'll regret once you're sober," Baron said.

Hunter pushed off the wall and took a step forward like he was looking to start something, but instead, he brushed passed Baron and headed toward his own cabin, "Pussy-whipped assholes, all of you."

Baron shook his head before heading to his own cabin. Something was up with Hunter, and if Baron didn't know Hunter, he'd have gone after him to see what exactly that was. However, his bullheaded baby cousin had never been one to budge on anything he wasn't ready to do. So, for now, he'd let him walk off and hopefully sober up. Hunter would come to him when he was ready and not a moment sooner.

Stepping into his house, Baron glanced at the clock on the wall and cursed. He hadn't realized just how late in the morning it actually was. He had just enough time to shower and make breakfast before he had to make his way down to the Cross Logging main office. While Bechet and Baron headed up the new Cross Furniture, Baron, being the oldest, had inherited the reigns of the main arm of the company. His father had insisted he work his way up from boots on the ground in the mountains, marking and felling trees to be brought down to processing, to loading trucks and processing orders out of the warehouse for hours on end.

That had been another thing Christine had hated—being the wife of a factory worker—even knowing he stood first in line to inherit the company from his father.

Baron didn't even want the job, but he'd grown up his entire life being groomed for it. He would much rather have kept working with his hands. At least then, he could be out on the mountain every day. Sitting in an office pushing paper just wasn't for him, but it was too late to back out. He was committed, not only to the family business but to helping his younger brothers turn the entire operation around, even if they doubted his sincerity on the matter. It was the least he could do in return for them helping him out of the massive financial hole Christine had left him in.

So yeah, that meant lots of hours processing paperwork and making sure they kept up their lumber production goals. Baron hadn't been given the keys to the entire castle just yet, and for that, he was grateful.

After going over the latest OSHA report for the factory for the fourth time, Baron checked his watch. It was hitting lunch, and he still couldn't make the jumble of words make sense to his brain. All he wanted to do was daydream about Genesis. It definitely wasn't helping that he couldn't seem to rid himself of her cherry and almond scent. Hell, it seemed to get stronger and stronger every time he was with her.

It was distracting.

She was a distraction.

One he didn't need, especially now that he finally had some fresh air to breathe without Christine and her toxic cloud hanging over him. He couldn't afford to commit himself to anyone or anything else right now, at least until the dust had settled. Genesis was a stranger in the ways it counted, and he sure as hell wasn't ready for another relationship. Had no idea when or if he ever would be. So, he used the time it took for him to walk back to the main house for lunch to put a mental fucking wall up around his heart. His job and mental health were his priority, and he was a dumb fuck for chasing pussy around the mountain instead of focusing on what he should.

Chapter Four

Genesis couldn't help the smile on her face as she pushed farther up the mountain. Her thighs burned with the extra exertion from last night on top of the hike. She really should have taken it easy, but she had no control when it came to Baron. Not just as Genesis, but her Bear seemed just as untamed when it came to him.

Last night, she'd marked him once more. A stronger mark than the previous night, and while she didn't want to think about what all that meant, she couldn't bring herself to feel guilty about it either. If she orgasmed, she scent marked. There was nothing voluntary about the action. It just was what it was. Her biological imperative to mark her territory, a temporary claim. In her previous sexual encounters, the mark had only lasted a few hours to a few days depending on the intensity or quantity of orgasms. Since Baron seemed perfectly yoked to bring her too many intense orgasms, it was no wonder her scent came out stronger, more potent when in his arms.

Genesis looked to the tops of the trees. The farther up she got on the mountain, the grander Sowell Gate rose before her. Her Bear railed against her, wanting to be let out, but after yesterday, Genesis would have to be more careful. Baron had been right about the growing danger of the terrain the closer they got to the gate. The trees were closer together, thick spiny underbrush blocking almost all pathways not already cut out by years of curious hikers.

Then there were the animals. Not just the actual animals either, that tended to stay far away from the main trail, but the others who were just outside of her visual range. The ones following her. She'd known there would be Shifters, had planned on it, but she knew better than to approach them first.

Wild or rogue Shifters weren't the friendliest bunch, and even though she'd planned to ask around about her parents, she was starting to get cold feet about the whole thing. What if her real father was out here still? What if he really was an asshole so dangerous her mother had risked everything to get her away from him? Genesis felt the panic rising in her chest, but she shoved it down. No need to alert them to her unease.

Instead, she pushed forward onto her next camp, just as the sun was blocked out by ominous grey clouds. Her research on the area had warned her about the sudden storms common around the gate, but there was something particularly troublesome in the air.

She set up her tent and checked her phone. The reception wasn't the best, but still enough to get her coordinates through to Baron via text. As soon as she slipped her phone back into her pocket, she heard rustling in the brush to her left.

Genesis turned toward the noise, not expecting to see anything in particular, but to her surprise, a large black Wolf emerged, followed by two others. Genesis stood her ground but didn't make any sudden movements. She held eye contact with the Wolf until his Alpha status forced her to look away.

The Wolf moved closer and sniffed at her before growling low. Genesis braced herself for an attack. She wouldn't shift just yet, in case that was interpreted as a sign of aggression on her part. Eventually, the Wolf and his buddies backed off, disappearing into the forest. Genesis remained on guard until she could no longer hear them.

Once they were gone, she stripped and shifted. Her Bear needed to run so she could get back to camp before the weather got any worse. But Genesis didn't get too far before she found herself surrounded again, this time not just by Wolves but other Shifters as well. She positioned herself for the fight she expected when one of the Bear Shifters came ambling forward and shifted into human form.

"We ain't here to fight unless you start something," he said.

Genesis shifted into human form as well. "I'm not looking to fight. I'm just passing through," she said.

The man looked her over, obvious lust in his eyes. He wasn't that bad-looking himself, tan skin and long wavy hair that brushed the top of his well-toned ass, yet her Bear wasn't having any of it. Even if he was one of her kind, she had an obvious preference for Baron. So, Genesis crossed her arms over her bare chest, obscuring his view of her body as best she could.

Nudity was common in the Shifter community, especially with those who preferred their animal forms and lived in the wild. Still, Genesis had been raised human, and any man so openly perusing her body without invitation made her feel uncomfortable, to say the least.

"You stink of human," he said.

"I was raised by them," she replied, and he recoiled.

"Such a waste. Maybe if you stick around, I can show you the true ways of our people," he said.

"Actually, that's kind of why I'm here. I'm not used to rogues banding together in such numbers. Are you the Alpha here?"

The man looked her over before scowling. "We are not rogue. We belong to the Sowell Gate Pack. Our Alpha is Yarrow Lupin, but he lets us on the mountain govern ourselves," he said.

"Okay, well, is he around somewhere?"

"I act in his stead up here. What do you wish to discuss?"?

"I came here in search of my lineage."

The Bear Shifter raised his eyebrow at her before coming closer. Genesis did her best not to lean or step back as he got well into her personal space. He sniffed a few times before his eyes fell to the dark purple birthmark between her shoulder blades. It was small and horseshoe-shaped; most people wouldn't notice it, but he did. The mark began to warm under his gaze, a gentle tingle of warmth that slowly grew into a blazing inferno the longer he gazed at it. She flinched when he touched it and took a step away. Confusion racked her brain as the burning sensation eased at his touch.

"I didn't give you permission to touch me," she snapped.

He smirked before moving his hair to the side and showing off a similar-shaped birthmark in the same place as hers. "I don't need permission to touch what is mine," he growled.

Genesis shook her head as the salty musk of the stranger's mating scent filled the surrounding air. "I don't belong to you or anyone, asshole."

"That mark on your back says you do," he snarled and grabbed at her.

Genesis dodged his advance, the calm before breaking as the other Shifters closed in tighter around her. Genesis wasn't the best fighter, and she surely wouldn't be able to take on so many. One thing was for sure, she was not about to let herself be forcibly mated, no matter what this stranger claimed. Thankfully, just before the man grabbed for her again, an elderly woman emerged from the crowd.

"Arthur, stop! You may be right about her marking, but it doesn't automatically make her your mate," the older woman snapped.

Arthur glared at the woman but didn't make a move against her or towards Genesis.

"She wears the mark. It's set-in-stone," he growled.

"The old ways are no longer upheld. This young lady has a choice. You want her, you court her properly, or I'll report you to Yarrow myself," the older woman said.

Arthur did not look happy with the woman, but he obviously wasn't going to risk the wrath of the Alpha. He gave Genesis's naked body one long look before he blew her a kiss.

"I will have you," he said darkly before shifting back into his Bear and running off.

Most of the drama over, the other Shifters took off as well, but the elderly woman stayed.

"Don't worry about Arthur, dear. He's been waiting a long time for you to show up," she said.

"I'm sorry, I have no idea what's going on."

"I knew Rebecca didn't agree with the practice, but I never thought she'd turn you over to humans to keep you out of it," the elderly woman said.

"You knew my mother?"

"Yes, I'm Betsy, your grandmother. Your father was my son, and your mother was human."

The initial shock of learning that this woman was her grandmother was tempered by her intense desire for answers. "Can you tell me what happened?"

Betsy looked to the ground. "It's a long story. Follow me."

Genesis was hesitant to follow the woman, especially as she turned further away from where she had set camp. The old woman claimed to be her grandmother, but so far, the Shifters in this area had shown her nothing but hostility. The sky grew darker, and the wind held a bitter chill that Genesis wasn't excited about. She was too far from camp to make it inside before the sky would break open and rain icy fresh hell on them. So she pushed down her concern and pushed forward.

"Come along, girl, an old woman like me needs to be inside for a storm like what's coming," her apparent grandmother said.

She fell into step next to the older woman. Betsy wasn't feeble in the least, and she cut through the forest with an efficiency born from decades of experience with the area.

We could have lived free!

We would have been forcefully mated to that douchebag Arthur.

No! We would have claimed our mate.

Do you need to run again because you sound a little cabin fever?

They stopped at what looked like a sheer cliff face emerging from the trees, and the elderly woman took her hand, walking them both straight through what looked like solid stone.

"What the...?"

The old lady smiled at her. "A little trick I learned from a witch I took as a lover in my youth," Betsy laughed.

"I didn't know there were witches too. I thought magic was a myth," Genesis said.

Betsy snorted. "Girl, how do you think we came about our animals, if not magic? Anyway, that's another story for another time. Let me start a fire before the temperature drops too low."

Genesis studied her surroundings as the old woman tossed a few logs into a small hearth and, with a snap or two of her fingers, set it ablaze. The new light source cast dancing shadows along the rock walls and across the minimal comforts the older woman kept. A sturdy wooden bed frame that sat low to the ground, a stool upon which she now sat, and a couple of pots for cooking.

Genesis could almost see herself as a young child sitting in front of that fire, listening to Betsy's stories on a cold day just like this one. Her gut twisted with hurt thinking about how much she would have loved that. Only now, she was an adult, and the story she longed for her grandmother to tell her wasn't a fairy tale with a happily ever after to brighten her day.

"Why did my mother leave?" Genesis asked.

"My son, Gunner, wasn't an easy man. He was always a little too wild, even for us out here on the mountain."

"So the letter wasn't lying; he did abuse her."

Betsy nodded her head. "Not physically, at least not at first. I don't know if he couldn't control his anger or if he just never tried to. Gunner liked to be in control of just about everything else. He treated your mother as a possession more than a person. I don't think she minded that too much until she had you. She might have been okay with it for herself, but you see, a mother always wants better for her children. She and I both thought Gunner would soften some once you were born. Instead, he got worse. When he attacked two humans in one of his rages, he was cast out as a rogue.

Arthur's family has always been close with the Alpha's, and Gunner wanted back into the Pack so he could make a run for Alpha himself. It was his quest for power that was his ultimate undoing. He sold you to Arthur's family. Had a warlock bind your fate with his in exchange for the family's support for him being reinstated in the Pack."

"He sold me? I'm bound to Arthur?"

"See, that's where things get complicated. The bond would only form if all terms of the deal were met. Gunner never got a chance to be reinstated because as soon as your mother found out what he'd done, she ran away with you. We all thought you were dead. Your mother told your father you were in a better place, made it seem like she'd killed you. He killed her in his rage, and then he, too, died of a broken heart. See, your parents were fated mates. That kind of bond is serious business."

Genesis could only stare at Betsy, trying to figure out if she was insane or not. "So, you thought I was dead this whole time?"

"Only at first. Arthur's family tracked down the warlock when Arthur's mark didn't disappear. The snake was able to tell us you were alive but not where you were. Wherever your mother took you was too far for him to see."

"Why didn't you come looking for me?"

Betsy gave Genesis a long look. "There are too many reasons to get into right now. Anyway, this storm is looking to be a bad one. You should stay here tonight," she said.

Genesis shook her head. Even with the storm that was going on outside. It was nothing compared to the one threatening to break loose inside of her. She needed time to wrap her head around the crazy Betsy had just dropped in her lap. "I'll be fine at my camp," she said and left.

Her apparent grandmother didn't follow or even try to change her mind. Maybe Genesis's mother had been right to tell her never to come back here. As much as this place had felt like home before, now all Genesis could think about was her parents' tragic demise. She wandered the woods, lost in her thoughts and eventually lost in the brush. She realized only after the ground was thoroughly blanketed with snow to the point that she had no way of remembering the way back to her own camp. She shifted into her Bear form to keep warm and did her best to retrace her steps.

Blizzard Warning in Effect for Shadowhaven, Edgewood, and Sowell Gate State Park...

Baron had to force himself not to speed on the quickly disappearing road back to Cross Estate. The snow fell faster now than when he'd left to go pick up the extra candles his mother had needed. The snow began to fall shortly after they had sat down for lunch. A light dusting at first, but his mother hadn't wanted to be caught off guard if it became another freak blizzard. He'd jumped at the chance to run the errand because of his need for more condoms just in case Genesis wanted another interlude at camp. Now here he was, acting a fool on the road because instead of worrying about getting home before the storm hit, he was now petrified about Genesis being trapped on the mountain in the coming weather.

He slammed the truck into park in front of the main house and dropped the pack of candles just inside the door before heading to the garage to grab the trail runner. He hoped he would be able to get up to Genesis's camp and back before the snow was too thick for the off-road vehicle.

"Whoa there, bud. Where do you think you're going?" Braxton said when he saw him pushing the off-roader out of the garage.

"My friend is still up on the mountain," he replied, desperate to be on his way to Genesis.

Braxton pinched the bridge of his nose, a pained expression on his face. "How far up?"

"Far enough for this to be a close one. Now get out of the way," Baron barked.

Braxton shook his head before stepping aside. "Hey! Send me the coordinates or something just in case you get stuck out there too!"

Baron was already speeding away, but he slowed enough to forward Genesis's text with her location to his brothers and Hunter. He felt his phone buzzing in his pocket, but he didn't bother to answer it. His focus was on getting to Genesis before it was too late. The trail that had been completely clear that morning was already getting hard to make out in the falling snow. Baron began to worry he might get stuck before he could make it to her.

He pushed the vehicle as hard as it could go given the conditions, and yet it didn't seem to matter. By the time he reached the end of the vehicle trail, there was already over a foot of snow on the trail. It was going to be a miracle for him to be able to make it to her and back.

CHAPTER FIVE

Genesis let out a sigh of relief as she finally reached her camp, she'd struggled to find it at first, but thankfully she'd been able to follow the few scent markers her Bear had left when she got close. She shifted into human form and cleared a path to her tent. She'd just slipped on her shirt when she sensed she wasn't alone. She slid into her pants and poked her head out. She smiled when she saw Baron come barreling into her camp.

"Hey! What are you doing here?" she asked, coming out of the tent.

Baron swept her into his arms and kissed her, rough and demanding. "Get your shit. I'm taking you home," he said when he finally let them both up for air.

Genesis smiled and shook her head. "It's just a little snow. I can manage."

She knew it was more than just a little snow, but she also didn't want to intrude on Baron, and yeah, the fact that he lived with his parents was a thing too. Baron scowled at her before marching over to her tent to grab her pack. While his head was in the tent, Genesis noticed movement along the perimeter of her camp. Too large and fast to be human. She sniffed the air and frowned. Arthur.

Baron came out of the tent, half of her things spilling out of her pack. "I got what looked important. We can come back for the rest of it later, but we gotta go, babe," Baron said.

Genesis opened her mouth to protest, but the loud roar of a pissed-off Bear rang through the air. Baron froze in shock.

"Shit," Genesis cursed.

Baron's eyes grew wide, and he moved quickly. Tossing her over his shoulder, he started moving back in the direction he came. Tossed over his shoulder, Genesis saw Arthur's Bear burst from cover. He was charging directly at them.

"Baron, put me down!"

"Fuck, no. We're getting out of here," Baron snapped, but it was too late.

Arthur's Bear tackled Baron to the ground, sending Genesis flying. Without thinking, Genesis shifted, not caring that her clothes would be ruined. She and her Bear had only one thing in mind. Protecting their mate. They tackled Arthur head-on, knocking him off Baron, who was curled into a ball, lying as still as he possibly could, blood leaking through the claw marks in his coat.

Genesis saw red, and her Bear roared in anger. Arthur charged again for Baron, but she blocked him with her body. They met in a clash of claws and teeth. Their Bears rolled away from Baron, locked in battle. Genesis knew this wasn't going to be as simple as chasing Arthur off. He'd gotten a taste of Baron's blood. It was clear his Bear wouldn't stop until Baron was dead, and that meant she would have to kill him or die trying.

Baron nearly shit his pants when he realized he was being attacked by a fucking Bear. If he died today, Baron wouldn't be the first Cross to fall victim to a Bear attack. His mind took him back to his Uncle's closed casket and his brother Braxton unconscious in the hospital, bandages wrapped around his slashed-up back. Then he'd been worried about Genesis. She hadn't uttered a peep since he'd thrown her as far as he could while he was falling. The Bear was no longer on top of him, but he could hear it still so close.

He dared a peek, and his eyes bugged, seeing not one but two Bears locked in a fierce battle. At least with the Bears occupying each other, he had a chance to get away with Genesis. He was injured, but not too bad. He could possibly carry her if she was hurt worse. He searched the snow-covered ground and quickly forgot all about the Bears when all he saw was Genesis's pack and her clothes shredded to pieces beside him.

"Genesis!" he whisper-yelled, crawling in the direction where he had thrown her. Maybe she'd made a run for it during the Bear attack.

He couldn't even be pissed about her leaving him for dead in this situation. He'd literally been tackled by a Bear. He didn't dare stand and risk bringing the Bear's attention back to him, but he got on his hands and knees and started to crawl. The Bears were still raging behind him, but all he could think about was getting back to his vehicle and hopefully finding Genesis safe.

Arthur's Bear fell with a heavy thud to the ground. He was still alive, but just barely. Genesis moved in for the kill, but the low growls of more Bears in the trees surrounding the clearing gave her pause. She was tired and weak from the injuries she'd sustained during the fight. If she killed Arthur now, the others were making it clear they wouldn't just let her go.

Her Bear slowly backed away from Arthur as the other Bears approached. Not just the Bears, but the Wolves as well. Their fight had not gone unnoticed, and neither had the reason for their altercation. Baron was on his hands and knees. He'd obviously tried to crawl away, but now he was stock still, face to face with a Wolf.

Genesis roared and charged. The Wolf growled low after sniffing the air. She knew the Wolf smelled her scent on Baron and didn't like it. Genesis prepared for another fight, despite knowing she'd probably not make it this time, but her Bear had other ideas. She moved quickly, putting herself in front of Baron and the Wolf. She looked into Baron's eyes; he was scared shitless, and she did her best to convey that she wasn't going to hurt him. His shocked expression turned to one of confusion, and that's when her Bear struck, sinking her teeth into Baron's shoulder.

"Fuck!" he shouted, but the bite was over quickly. Genesis was shocked herself. She had no idea why her Bear would do such a thing, but deep down, she knew it wasn't to harm Baron but to mark him once and for all as theirs.

The rest of the Shifters seemed to understand this too. They let out a series of howls and roars before they slowly dispersed back into the woods. Unfortunately, her Bear decided to go as well, forcing her to shift right there in front of Baron.

Baron must be on the verge of death. He'd hallucinated seeing Genesis's eyes in the Bear's just before it bit the fuck out of his shoulder. Now he was hallucinating that same Bear turning into Genesis right before his eyes. Maybe it was the blood loss combined with the shock of it all, but for damn sure, it couldn't be real.

She couldn't be real.

Her arms circled his chest, and she pulled him upright. "Baron? Baron! I need you to stay with me. Please, at least until we get to your vehicle, okay?"

He nodded dumbly, gathering as much of his strength as he could to get to his feet. He had to lean heavily on Genesis, but she managed to get them both to the trail runner just as Hunter rolled up on his snowmobile.

"What the fuck happened?" He was off his vehicle and rushing to take Baron's weight from Genesis's naked frame.

Fuck, she was naked. She had carried his ass through the snow naked. He couldn't feel any more of an ass than he already did, except the loss of blood had everything fading fast.

Genesis suddenly became aware that she was still naked, the cold seeping into her skin with the loss of Baron's heat and the adrenaline. She wrapped her arms around herself and started to shiver. With the intrusion of the cold came the realization that not all of her wounds had healed during her shift. The man who had shouldered Baron cursed and shrugged out of his coat.

"Hi! I'm Hunter. Where the fuck are your clothes, woman?" then, "Shit, you okay to drive the trail runner? 'Cause I can only take one on the snowmobile."

Genesis took a deep breath, shrugging into the man's coat. "Yes, I think I can make it," she said.

"You think, or you're sure because my cousin isn't going to like it if he wasted his time trying to rescue you."

"I'm sure!" she said with a little more force than entirely necessary before climbing onto the trail runner.

"Alright, follow me, the snow seems to be lightening up, but it's going to be rough getting back to the estate," the man, who she now presumed was related to Baron, said.

"Let's just go," Genesis said.

Baron's cousin didn't waste any time. He hopped onto his snowmobile and took off. Genesis almost lost him a few times, but thankfully, like he said, the snow wasn't falling as heavily as before, and the farther down the mountain they got, the warmer the air. Unfortunately, that also meant the slicker the trail had become, and Genesis barely missed hitting the back of the snowmobile when it finally did slow down for her to catch up.

"I am not letting Aunt Melinda see either of you like this, so we are going to Baron's place," the man said when they parked out front of a massive log structure that resembled a hunting lodge more than an actual home.

Genesis followed the man as he carried Baron down a cleared pathway to a cozy-looking cottage. Not at all where she expected a man like Baron to live, but maybe this style choice had been made by his ex-wife. She didn't dwell on it long, especially once they were inside and out of the blistering cold.

"I'm Genesis, by the way. Thanks for lending me your coat," she said belatedly.

The man turned at her wild-eyed after he lay Baron out on the couch. "Hunter, Baron's cousin, and I'd like to know what the fuck happened out there, 'cause this shit ain't normal," he said, gesturing towards Baron's fresh wounds.

"We were attacked by Bears."

Baron's cousin paled. "What is with this family and fucking Bears?" Hunter grumbled.

"What was that?" Genesis asked, her interest piqued.

"Nothing. Why are you ass naked?" Hunter asked, obviously not going to elaborate on his Bear comment.

"I thought your cousin was coming to seduce me again, not rescue my ass from a little bit of snow. How were we supposed to know a fucking crazed Bear would attack?" Genesis said. She wasn't exactly lying to Baron's cousin, but there was no way she was going to tell him the truth. That she was the Bear who bit Baron and that it was her crazed Bear Shifter, almost fiancé, that had attacked them in a fit of jealous rage.

Hunter had the nerve to chuckle before his eyes softened a little. "Baron should have been more careful. He knows our family ain't supposed to be up there unprotected. You hurt?"

"Not as bad as Baron. He pushed me out of the way, taking most of the attack," she said.

Hunter cursed and undressed Baron to get a better look at his wounds. "Go get cleaned up. The bedroom is the door at the end of the hall. Baron won't mind if you borrow some clothes until we can get your stuff from the mountain," he said, not even looking at her.

"Are you a doctor?"

"Fuck no, but I've been in enough bar fights to know if a beating and cuts are hospital-worthy. He's gonna need a rabies shot for that bite, though," Hunter muttered.

Genesis didn't want to leave Baron's side, but she also didn't want to just stand there naked while his cousin tended to his wounds. She found Baron's bedroom just like Hunter said and sighed. The front room had small aspects of Baron, but this room—the massive bed with thick flannel sheets and no-frills décor—was more his style. Just a simple side table and a dresser tucked under a window that gave a view of the mountain.

She went to the dresser and opened the top drawer. Inside she found undershirts and boxers. She snagged one of his undershirts before moving to the next drawer. This one held a couple pairs of pajama bottoms and basketball shorts. She reached for the pajamas that looked more like sweats. Baron was a big man, but she had ass enough that with a little help from the drawstring and cuffing the bottom, they would work. Then she headed to open one of the two doors along the sidewall. The first turned out to be a massive closet. Only one small section held clothes. The rest was completely empty. Another sign that his ex-wife had tailored this place to her needs.

Judging by the amount of space in the closet, it came as no surprise that the bathroom would be heavenly. Sure enough, it looked more like a private spa than a home bath. There was a large jetted jacuzzi tub that could fit three Barons, a dual-headed shower stall that took up most of the back wall, a private water closet, his and her vanities that rivaled the size of most people's dual sink setups, and a steam room.

Everything was white, modern, and while practical in layout, it was nothing one would expect from the cozy cottage exterior. Genesis took a quick shower, and when she stepped out, she realized the floor was heated, keeping her toes nice and toasty, despite the marble tile beneath her feet. She moved over to the empty vanity and looked at herself in the mirror. Her cheek was bruised, among other things, but aside from a few nicks, most of her wounds had already started to heal. She took a deep breath and winced. Okay, maybe that wasn't all. She pressed at her ribs, finding a few not quite in the right position.

"Fucker dislocated my ribs," she hissed to herself.

She stepped back from the vanity. Her Bear wasn't going to like this, but there was no way she was going to suffer the weeks it would take to heal all the way. They could both share the pain, and thankfully, Baron's bathroom was large enough to accommodate her Bear for a very short period. Genesis tried to shift, but her Bear resisted. She tried again, and still nothing. Her Bear was being a stubborn bitch, but the need to make sure Baron was okay overrode her need to heal herself, so she shrugged into her borrowed clothes and made her way back to the front room.

Hunter stood when she entered the room. "I'm gonna need your help to get him to the shower. We need to clean him up before I can bandage him up," Hunter said.

"I told you, I'm not that broke; I can walk," Baron grumbled from the couch, but Genesis could hear the weakness in his voice.

She rushed over and sank to her knees next to him. "Listen, asshole, I already carried your heavy ass through the fucking woods, in the snow, after a Bear attack, while naked. Now is not the time to play or get all toxic with the masculinity, alright?" she said.

Baron had the nerve to smirk before kissing her. "Are you wearing my pajamas?"

Genesis rolled her eyes and grabbed Baron's arm. "Let's get him cleaned up before he passes out again," she said.

Hunter shook his head before taking Baron's other arm. Together, they got him into the bathroom.

"Shower or tub?" Genesis asked.

"Shower. Not sure I could lift his heavy ass enough to get him out," Hunter said.

They maneuvered Baron over to the shower. He was already undressed down to his boxers, but they left those on as they held him up under the spray. The drains ran red with his blood, and Genesis felt fury bubbling under the surface: at Arthur, the asshole, and also at herself for getting Baron caught up in her mess.

"That bite looks nasty, it's definitely going to scar, but man, is he lucky the Bear didn't go for the throat," Hunter winced.

Genesis bit her lip; she didn't need the extra guilt, but it was there, heavy on her shoulders. Not once, since finding out she was a Shifter, had Genesis ever felt like her life would be better without her Bear. Until now, seeing Baron loopy and weak from blood loss. From an injury she caused.

Arthur had done his own damage, but thanks to Baron's thick winter clothes, Arthur's claw marks had only just gone deep enough to draw blood. They'd be scabbed over in a matter of days, but her bite, no, her bite was much deeper and gnarly looking. He would definitely be left with a permanent scar; it might even get infected if not properly treated.

Once Baron was cleaned up, they sat him on one of the stairs leading up to the tub. Baron rested his head against Genesis's stomach, his arms wrapped around her waist.

"I thought I lost you," he said.

"You didn't lose me, Baron. There was nothing to lose," she said.

His grip on her tightened. "I know I'm not supposed to care. You were just supposed to be a little fun to celebrate my divorce."

"I know, and it's okay. Just let your cousin fix you up," she encouraged.

Hunter glared at her while he cut another piece of gauze to layer over Baron's wound.

"You don't understand. I wasn't supposed to care, but I realized during the attack that I did care. I care a whole hell of a lot, and it's crazy because I don't know you, and we only just met."

Genesis kissed him to get him to shut up, to stop talking before he said something he would regret later. Something that would make her eventual exit from his life hurt more than it already would.

She knew for a fact Baron was her mate.

She had tried to deny it, blaming her intense orgasms on the excess of marking pheromone she released every time they were together, but after her Bear literally marked him, Genesis knew there was no turning back from that. Not for her and not for Baron, but she wouldn't force him, couldn't force him into her life.

So, she kissed him with all the emotion she'd tried to hold back, knowing that once the roads were clear, she would be gone.

Chapter Six

As hot as her kiss was, it felt like goodbye. Baron didn't want goodbye. He wanted Genesis. He shouldn't want her like this, but he did. Being so close to death, his life flashing before his eyes, he asked for more time, not to be with family or to meet his career goals, but to have more time with Genesis. He should probably go see his therapist about it, but that was the truth of it.

If he survived this night, he would make his intentions clear with Genesis. He was very open to the idea of her sticking around as his woman. Not as a divorce gift to himself, not as a casual fuck buddy, but as his girlfriend. Whatever that would look like for them.

"Let me finish this, and then y'all two can finish," Hunter snapped, tugging at Baron's arm.

Baron pulled away from Genesis to glare at his cousin, but the quick head movement only made the world begin to spin. Genesis caught him against her body with a chuckle.

"Careful now. Let your cousin patch you up. You got any soda or juice in your fridge? You might need some sugar before you pass out again," Genesis said.

"Only sugar I need is right here," Baron said, grabbing her ass.

"Alright, I'm done. Let's get you to the couch. You've got a knot on your head, and I don't want you taking a forever nap while I get you some juice and soup from the main house," Hunter said.

Hunter helped Genesis get Baron back to the couch. They turned on the TV, and Hunter left to get the promised food. Genesis snuggled on the couch with Baron, a thick blanket wrapped around both of them. Baron had never considered himself the cuddling type, but now with Genesis's warm body cocooned with his, he was starting to see the appeal. He rested his head against the soft pillows of her bosom, his back couched between her legs, reminding him of their first sexual encounter. Her mounting him in a naughty game of horse before she rode his back to sticky sweet completion. His dick hardened at the thought, and he reached up with his good arm to take her hand and guide it right over the bulge in the pants she'd helped him get into earlier.

Genesis chuckled and gave him a gentle squeeze. "Not right now, Baron. Your cousin will be back any moment," she sighed.

Baron grunted. "I can make it quick," he said.

He tried to turn to face her but winced as the movement tugged on his wound.

Genesis wiggled out from under him and made him sit all the way up. "You are in no condition to do anything but rest right now. So, find something you'd like to watch until Hunter gets back."

"I'd like to watch you cum on my dick," he said, and she rolled her eyes before standing.

"On TV, Baron."

She moved away from the couch and into the kitchen. Baron had plenty of food and stuff in his own house. There had been no reason for Hunter to go to the main house to get food, except to gossip with the rest of the family about Baron and Genesis. The fact he was taking so long to get back only confirmed that for Baron. He was in no mood to watch TV, so he angled himself on the couch to watch Genesis as she moved around his kitchen. He noticed when it dawned on her, too. That there had been zero reason for Hunter to go get food from the main house. With a shake of her head, she pulled out a pot and a can of soup before moving to the stove to heat it up.

Her movements seemed so natural. Seeing her working her way around his kitchen, busily fixing him a meal, sent all sorts of warm and fuzzy feelings through his body. If she looked up at him now, Baron was certain she'd see little cartoon hearts floating over his head. It brought a flush to his cheeks and tightness to his loins. Almost as if his mind, heart, and dick were in sudden alignment over their need for her, for Genesis. He'd never felt anything quite like it and wasn't sure he was entirely opposed to it either. He hadn't sought to feel anything other than lust with Genesis, and while he couldn't call what he was feeling love, the potential for it to grow to that was there.

"Since you obviously aren't into watching TV, maybe you'd prefer to talk?"

Baron sighed, her question bringing him back to the present and away from the what-ifs of their future together. Talking was an option, but there wasn't a single question he really wanted the answer to that would do anything more than start trouble. Especially if she was still trying to keep things casual between them. He couldn't allow himself to read too much into the way she was caring for him right now. These were obviously not the circumstances for that. "Not really," he replied.

Genesis poured the can of soup into the pot and lit the burner. "Let's start simple then. What's your favorite color?"

"Brown," Baron groaned.

She looked around the room and smirked. "Well, that explains a few things. Mine is black," she said.

"Black?" Baron repeated.

"Yes, it's mysterious and goes with just about every other color."

"Black is literally the absence of color," he frowned.

"Hey! I didn't judge you for liking the color of poop, so you don't get to judge my color of choice either," she said, reaching for the spoon in the crock of utensils by the stove. She gave the soup a stir before moving to the cabinet where she had spotted the dishes earlier. She made a show of holding up the brown ceramic bowls before setting them on the counter.

"That's called burnt umber, and the utensils are in the drawer below," he said.

She opened the drawer and smiled. "Okay, I was so going to make fun of your burnt poop dishes, but these are amazing," She said, holding up one of the spoons. The eating surface was stainless steel, but the handle was hand whittled by Braxton. It was one of the first projects Baron had commissioned from his little bro when it became clear that woodworking was more Braxton's thing than chopping down trees.

"My brother Braxton made those for me. He's super talented."

"I agree. Look at how detailed the little squirrels are! Don't tell me your favorite animal is the squirrel because I will not let you live that down. They are basically little cheek-stuffing rats," she said.

"First of all, that may be true, but come on, they are adorable. Second, no, they are not my favorite. He picked random woodland creatures for each type of utensil. The spoons have Squirrels, the forks have Falcons, steak knives have Wolves, and the butter knives have Bears," he explained.

Genesis opened the drawer again and studied the different carvings on the utensils until the pot of soup began to boil over. With a curse, she slammed the drawer shut and rushed to turn off the stove.

"Sorry, I got distracted by the cuteness of your cutlery," she said.

Baron shook his head and tried to stand to help her, but his body refused to get with the program. He broke out in a light sweat just from the effort of heaving his body off the couch, only to immediately feel dizzy and flop back down.

"Fuck," he ground out in frustration.

Genesis was instantly by his side, her hands cupping his cheeks, concern in her eyes. "I told you not to move, okay? You need to rest. Just don't fall asleep, okay?" she said.

Baron leaned forward and pressed a soft kiss to her lips. "I hate feeling weak, feeling so helpless. Especially after..." he trailed off.

Genesis shook her head. "We don't have to talk about what happened on the mountain right now. Just relax and let me make sure you are okay. The sooner you do, the sooner you'll be back to feeling like yourself, I promise."

She returned his kiss, but this time he didn't let it end at a soft press of lips. She was already practically in his lap, so he tugged her all the way there and swept his tongue over her lips in a teasing manner. The concern evaporated from her gaze, replaced with heat and a want that Baron was all too ready to indulge.

Genesis had given up trying to stop whatever crazy awkward sex was about to happen between her and Baron. He was so thick and hard, his cock pressed against her ass. His hot tongue plunged into her mouth, caressing the roof of her mouth and dueling with her tongue.

She sipped at his lips and wiggled her ass over his erection, eliciting a frustrated groan from him.

"If you'd just... I could pull... pants down... get inside..." Snippets of his sentences were cut off by their kisses.

She wanted to let him. Her own core dripped with anticipation of him being inside of her, but then she heard someone stomping up the front porch, louder than necessary. Hunter, signaling he was about to come inside, kindly forewarning them to wrap up whatever shenanigans were underway.

"Go away, Hunter!" Baron growled, but Genesis was already off his lap and moving toward the door.

She opened it wide, surprised to find not just Hunter at the door but two other massive men outside the door.

"Um, hi," Genesis said, completely overwhelmed by the sheer magnitude of hot loggers standing in front of her.

Of course, Baron was her preference, but obviously, being his family, they shared similar features. She did her best not to fan herself as they barged into the small front room, dwarfing nearly everything in their presence. Everything except Baron, of course, who sat on the couch scowling at the three men.

For a moment, Genesis hung out by the door, unsure if she should disappear into Baron's bedroom so he could chat without her or stay in case he needed her help. She didn't think the men were here to do any further damage, but seeing Baron so weak and helpless on the couch made her protective instincts go on red alert.

She couldn't leave her mate in such a vulnerable position. Her Mate. With a capital M. As much as the designation excited her, it also sparked a pang of guilt and despair as to what that could mean in the future. She would have to come clean to Baron sooner rather than later. Should have said something about her Shifter status instead of rambling about her favorite colors and cutlery. Yet, the time for that had passed the moment she'd straddled his lap. Her lust for Baron, the urge to find the completion of their mating through more pleasurable means was stronger than her guilt at that moment. If his family hadn't just arrived, who knew if she'd have hurt him further. If she'd had found the time between orgasms to admit her truth.

Whatever may have come, it didn't matter now as the three massive men stood in front of Baron on the couch. Baron looked pissed about their intrusion and scowled hard at the trio. All the men seemed to have forgotten she was there as they took in the sight of Baron pale and obviously weak on the couch. Genesis pressed her back against the wall and watched as their dynamic unfolded before her. She had a feeling she would need this insight in the future when it came down to who she could trust with Baron's best interest in mind.

It wasn't the first time Baron's younger brothers and cousin had interrupted him in the middle of something, but that didn't stop it from being any less aggravating. He glared at the three men he had some hand in raising and did his best to put some bass in his voice. He might be okay with letting Genesis see him a little out of it—even Hunter since he'd been the only one around during the darker days of his marriage—but not his little brothers. Especially not Bechet, who had always had this holier-than-thou attitude and scoffed at Baron for wanting to uphold the family legacy.

"Hunter, where is the soup you were supposed to bring? Bechet, when did you get out here? Braxton, you better not go telling your wife all my business."

"Shut up, Baron. We're here to help Hunter bring you and your friend back to the main house. As soon as Mother heard you two got attacked by a fucking Bear, she was adamant on all of us being up at the main house until the blizzard was over," Bechet said.

"Yeah, thanks for that. I promised Carmen that wasn't happening this year; way to make me the asshole," Braxton said.

"Why the fuck did you tell her about the Bear?" he asked Hunter.

"Like they wouldn't know after seeing the mess on your shoulder? Hell, you're lucky you still have a fucking arm and can move it," Hunter replied.

"Don't get mad at Hunter for telling us the truth. I swear, Baron, for being the oldest, you sure have a way of forgetting all your responsibilities over some pussy," Bechet said.

Baron was ready to launch off the couch at his little brother, but Genesis got in his way. "I don't give a fuck who you are, but this *pussy* will kick your motherfucking ass if you don't either show some fucking compassion or get the fuck out."

Genesis was right in Bechet's face, even with the height difference. Baron grabbed Genesis's hand and tugged her back.

"I don't need you fighting for me," he said, and she turned her glare at him before tossing her hands in the air.

"You are in no condition to be dealing with this kind of nonsense, and I'm not going to allow it to continue, so you shut up and let me handle this." She turned back to his brothers and crossed her arms over her chest. "Hunter and I barely got him from this couch to the bathroom and back. Now y'all want to drag him back out into the cold? I think the fuck not. Send my apologies to your mother, but we'll be fine here until the morning. Now. All of you. Out!" she said.

The three large men looked stunned for a moment before peeking around to shoot questioning looks at Baron.

"You heard her; get out," he said.

Hunter let out a long low whistle. "Alright, but I'm totally throwing you both under the bus with Aunt Melinda. Good luck with that," Hunter said before tipping an imaginary hat and heading for the door.

Bechet followed, but Braxton lingered. Unlike Bechet, Braxton had actually mellowed out after getting married and, over the last year, had stepped in as the voice of reason in some of their brotherly discussions.

"What, Braxton?"

"I'm just glad you are both safe and back home. Get some rest and, um, maybe be fully clothed by noon? I'll try to stall the womenfolk as long as I can, but it took us quite a while to convince them not to come by tonight," Braxton said.

Baron nodded. "Thanks, bro."

Braxton nodded back and headed out the door. He was finally alone with Genesis again, but the mood had definitely shifted. Not just his mood but hers as well. He could see the spark of anger dimming to be replaced with an almost haunted look. The rose-colored glasses of lust had faded as he took in the bruising on her cheek and the stilted way she moved her body.

Asshole! You didn't even ask if she was okay.

"I'll serve you some soup, and then after another thirty minutes or so, we'll get you to bed," she muttered before moving back to the stove.

Baron pushed himself into a more seated position. It was the most he could do at this point.

"Don't worry about all that, Genesis. Come rest. Tonight has to have been a lot for you too," he said.

She didn't look up at him. She remained focused on filling the two bowls she had pulled out with soup. She brought both over to the couch before she spoke. "I think the adrenaline is finally wearing off. Let's eat, and then maybe we can make it to the bed before we both crash too hard."

Baron hated that she was still refusing to look at him. It made the pain in his shoulder ten times worse. Like someone had just doused the whole thing with alcohol and set it ablaze. It defied logic, but he wasn't in a position to deny what his body felt at the moment. He gritted his teeth to keep from crying out. Genesis had done enough for him tonight. He could tough out the pain.

Genesis was so focused on avoiding his gaze that it took her a moment to realize he wasn't eating. She set her own spoon down and picked up his bowl. Her gaze finally met his again when she brought a spoonful to his lips. "Eat, Baron."

He opened his mouth, accepting the spoonful, and although he knew it was just regular old chicken and stars, somehow it tasted like heaven. The warm liquid slid down his throat and doused the flames on his shoulder. It was then that he knew something about his attraction to Genesis wasn't normal. That there were forces at work he couldn't possibly comprehend, and he didn't exactly know how to feel about that.

Chapter Seven

S he couldn't breathe. The pain in her side was too intense, yet she didn't want to move and risk waking Baron. His heavy arm trapped her in place and pressed right on top of her dislocated ribs. She grabbed his finger and did her best to gently move his arm lower without impaling her lungs on a broken bone. Last night with all the bruising and inflammation, her ribs had only felt dislocated, but now in the morning, she knew at least three of them were broken. It was the only explanation for the ridiculous amount of pain she was in.

Genesis silently cursed her Bear for not wanting to help her heal. If this was some fucked up way of getting her to stay with Baron longer, her Bear was going to be sorely disappointed. Mate or not, she wasn't going to force her way into Baron's life. It wasn't right. Not just because of the circumstances that had brought them to that point but because, frankly, neither of them was ready for that kind of commitment.

Baron was fresh off a divorce. And Genesis? She had too much going on in her life to bring anyone else into it. Not to mention she had no understanding of how she was supposed to handle mating a human. Her mentor had always warned her against it. The few other Shifters she'd come across in her life had also been very clear that humans were for play, not for forever. Both had stressed the importance of never telling a human the truth about supernaturals being real.

Yet, here she was mated to Baron. A human who had no idea about the supernatural elements around him. Even knowing what she knew about her own parents didn't give her any hope of a real future with Baron. How would he handle knowing? Would he hate her for her lies of omission? Would he think her crazy? Baron hadn't struck her as the type to believe in anything he couldn't put easily into a standard box. So she was basically screwed. He deserved the truth from her, even if it meant he'd walk away.

Her decision made, Genesis tried to shimmy her way out of bed, slower this time so as not to jostle her broken body. Baron's grip tightened on her waist, further trapping her on the bed and forcing another wave of pain through her chest. His morning wood pressed along the crease of her ass, growing thicker and longer by the second. He was awake in more ways than one. If she weren't in so much pain, she would make quick work of putting their desires to bed.

"Good morning, Baron," she wheezed.

His grip loosened enough for him to roll her onto her back. His eyes were full of concern. "Are you okay?"

She smiled and nodded. "Yeah, are you?"

Baron rolled his shoulder and winced. "It hurts like a bitch, but I'll be alright," he said before leaning down to kiss her.

His body pressed into hers, and as much as she had previously enjoyed the press of his massive body against hers, today, it was just too painful. She shoved at his chest. "Fuck, ouch! Stop!"

Baron moved away from her and frowned before tossing the covers from her. She was naked, and the bruising on her ribcage was clear as day, even if it was already fading in places.

"Genesis," he sighed before placing gentle kisses across her mottled skin.

Genesis moaned with pleasure, grateful his kisses felt like a soothing balm to her aches.

"Okay, so I may have dislocated and or broken a rib or two, but I'm fine," she said.

He straightened, sitting up immediately. Concern was clear on his face, even through the slight grimace he made as he tweaked his own injuries.

"You are not fine. You shouldn't have been moving me around at all last night. You could have a punctured lung," he said.

She could tell Baron was pissed at her but fuck if she didn't find it adorable. Everything, from the pinch of his thick eyebrows to the thinning of his lips, only made her want to squeeze his cheeks and tease a smile out of him.

"If I'd punctured a lung, I'd know. I promise to be more careful while it's healing, but last night, you were the priority," she said.

"Fuck that! I didn't rush all the way up that mountain and face off with a Wolf and a Bear just for you to collapse a lung in my bed," he said.

"Baron, calm down. I'm okay. We're both okay." She was going for soothing, but she could see in his eyes that he was reliving last night's events.

"Fuck, I was so far gone last night. I thought the Bear turned into you," he said, rubbing a hand over his face.

Genesis bit her lip and looked away from him. Her Bear was screaming for her to tell him the truth. To explain what she was and why she bit him, but her human half was not having it. It was bad enough they had mated him without consent, but he'd nearly died because of her. Then again, letting him think he'd lost his mind wasn't an appealing option either.

"About that," she said, pushing herself into a seated position. "You weren't hallucinating."

Baron eyed her like she'd grown three heads right in front of him, but she continued explaining. She told him about her first shift, finding her mentor, and why she'd been so adamant about hiking alone in the mountains. He didn't say a single word as she laid everything out on the table. About Arthur, about herself, and about the bite.

"I am so sorry. I didn't expect any of this to happen. If you want me to leave, if you never want to see me again, I understand, but you deserve the truth, Baron," she finished.

He was no longer sitting close to her in bed. He'd moved clear to the other side of the room, leaning against the wall and staring at her. Just staring. Not saying a word; barely breathing; just staring. Genesis looked away as tears formed in her eyes. This was it. This was exactly what she expected to happen. He either believed her and was scared out of his mind, or he didn't and thought she was batshit crazy.

She tilted her head to look out the window—anything to avoid looking at him—the snow had stopped, and the sun was out. The blizzard hadn't been as bad as everyone had expected, and the white blanket atop the roof was already beginning to melt. She climbed out of bed, not bothering to get dressed. She didn't have any clothes of her own, and it was early enough that she could probably shift and make it to the line of trees without being spotted.

"Thank you for coming to find me, Baron, and for the other night," she said before opening the bedroom door and leaving.

Baron didn't believe a word she'd said. At least, not at first. Not when she'd first said she was a Shifter. That she was a Bear Shifter and had bitten him. It was when he looked at her and saw her eyes flash golden. Even though Genesis spoke, he could see there was someone or something else there as well. He found himself pressed against the wall in shock and partial fear that while he could trust Genesis, he had no idea what damage could befall him and his family if he couldn't trust the other part of her.

He tried to organize his thoughts a bit before he formulating words. His entire body had frozen in place with the effort to wrap his head around things, but when he could finally function, she was gone. Her absence registered sharply like a kick in the gut. The world swam for a moment, and when he righted himself, she appeared outside his bedroom window. Naked as sin, walking through the snow like she wasn't freezing her ass off, and then it happened. Her body contorted unnaturally, and then she fell onto all fours. Genesis was gone, and in her place was a Bear, the same size and color as the one who'd bitten him last night.

The Bear roared, looking directly at his cottage before taking off into the woods. The bite on his shoulder began to throb so fiercely that he thought his whole arm would fall off, but it was nothing compared to the vice grip around his heart.

She'd told him her truth, and it hadn't changed how he felt about her. Yet he'd taken too long to reach that conclusion. Genesis had to know how he felt before she slipped out of his hands forever. The pain in his shoulder worsened, and he took a few deep breaths, settling into the rhythm he'd learned to help calm himself during the dark time. When the storm inside him settled and the pain in his shoulder lessened, Baron threw on his clothes and headed to the garage. Baron had no idea what his plan was if and when he found Genesis, but he knew he couldn't let her leave like this.

CHAPTER EIGHT

Genesis was known to run from things in her life, but this time her Bear wasn't a willing participant. Although she allowed Genesis to shift and heal herself, the Bear did nothing to help ease the pain of the transition. Genesis felt every single crack and contortion of her bones and muscles all three times it took to heal her ribs. The pain of shifting was nothing compared to the searing dagger stuck in her heart. It wasn't like she hadn't expected this outcome, but that didn't make it any easier. Somehow, she'd managed to fall for Baron in just a few days, and now not only was she heartbroken, but her Bear was pissed at her as well.

You shouldn't leave!

He doesn't want us.

You didn't give him a chance!

A chance? Really? Like you gave him any choice? What were you thinking marking him like that?

Her Bear let out a frustrated roar before shutting Genesis out completely.

Yeah, that's what I thought, and normally you're the one chastising me for leading with my pussy!

The Bear's silent treatment was welcome as she pushed the last mile to her abandoned camp. Both Genesis and her Bear were too into their own heads to register the presence of outsiders in the camp until it was too late for any pretense of caution. Genesis shifted back to human form and approached the three new Shifters rummaging through her things.

"Who the fuck are you, and what are you doing with my property?" she spat.

The three men looked up at her. One smirked, one shrugged, and the other shot her a glare. "You the rogue causing all the drama?" he asked.

Genesis rolled her eyes and snatched her bag out of the man's hands. She pulled out a new shirt and pulled it over her body. It did nothing to stop the chill of the mountain air from settling in, nor did the thin t-shirt do anything to hide the hard peaks of her frigid nipples, but at least she wasn't stark naked in front of three strangers.

"I don't answer to nameless strangers," she spat.

The guy had the nerve to smirk before introducing himself. "I'm Calix, and those two are Jacinto and Florian. We are enforcers for the Sowell Gate Pack."

Genesis nodded in acknowledgment of their status in the local pack, but that was all the care she could give at the moment. Right now, all she wanted was to get her stuff and get the hell off this mountain before anything else went wrong.

"There ain't no drama here. Now excuse me. I think I'll be on my way," she said and tried to brush past the rude one.

He grabbed her arm, firm but not enough to hurt her. "Listen, we're generally cool with rogues in our territory as long as they lie low. Attacking one of our leadership is a punishable offense," Calix growled.

"Your leadership tried to force a mating claim on me and then attacked my human mate. So, fuck you and him. I hope he died for the audacity," she replied.

The man's eyes darkened, and he sniffed around her. Then let her arm go. "There was human blood on the trail. Is your mate going to recover?"

"Physically, yes. He didn't know Shifters existed until last night," Genesis sighed.

"You saying Arthur exposed himself to your mate, whom you hadn't told you were a Shifter?"

"My mate and I just met earlier this week. I wasn't exactly in the oh, by the way, I'm a Bear Shifter stage, okay??"

"If Arthur exposed himself to a human, he deserved to get his ass whooped," Florian or Jacinto said. Calix hadn't exactly specified which of his backup was which.

Genesis allowed a moment to laugh before sobering. As much as she would love to pin everything on that asshole Arthur, she had to admit her own responsibility for what went down, "He didn't see Arthur shift, but I couldn't hold my Bear form after the fight. I was raised by humans. I'm not that great at controlling my Bear form for long, especially when I'm amped up or in pain."

"Fuck, man, this shit just keeps getting worse," the other enforcer said.

The three enforcers seemed to be considering how to handle the issue, but Genesis wasn't going to wait for them to make a final verdict. "Anyway, I get that y'all don't want me around, and I'll be out of your hair by this afternoon," she said and started to take down her tent.

"Not okay. You need to be brought to the Alpha. I'll allow you to gather your shit, but then you are coming with us," Calix said.

"Right, that Yarrow Lupin guy. Arthur mentioned him briefly before he went full asshole."

"Just hurry up and get your shit," the guy snapped.

Genesis rolled her eyes and grumbled the whole time, but she couldn't honestly be upset when she was getting a free ride into Sowell City instead of having to walk it or hitchhike. What Genesis hadn't expected was for Baron to come barreling into the clearing.

"She ain't going nowhere but home with me," he growled.

She might have swooned a little at his show of protection if she didn't know just how vastly unmatched he was to three Shifter males. Pack enforcers, if she was getting the vibe right. To their credit, not a single one of them moved to hurt Baron or even restrain him as he came to stand by her side.

"Baron, what are you doing here?" she asked.

He glared at her for a moment before cursing. "You dropped a whole lot of crazy on my lap and then up and left. You think that's any way to have a conversation?" he snapped.

Genesis couldn't help it. She burst into a fit of giggles. "A conversation? Really?"

"Yeah, I have questions. Lots of 'em, and before you disappear, I want answers," he said.

She shook her head. "No further explanation is needed if you don't want me around. I told you what you needed to know so you wouldn't end up in some looney bin trying to sort it all out yourself," she said.

"Not good enough," he said.

"Listen, you two can have all the time in the world to have this conversation later, but I've got shit to do, and the Alpha is waiting," the asshole enforcer said.

The rest of the crew already held the rest of her gear. She turned to Baron and kissed him. "Go home, Baron. I'll call you," she said.

"Like hell, you will. Do you think I'm just going to let you go wherever with these assholes? No, I'm coming with," he said.

"That's not..."

The asshole enforcer cut her off. "He's your mate and part of the incident. He can come. Just let's go," he snapped.

Baron pulled Genesis against him, but gently enough not to make her injured ribs worse. Ribs that were still sore but no longer dislocated after multiple shifts from Bear to human and back. They hopped in another trail vehicle and took that down to the bottom of the trail, where a black SUV waited. The drive took them not to Sowell City, as Genesis had hoped, but to a smaller trailer village that Baron told her was called Sullah.

A large man with waist-length locs stood in the middle of the clearing next to a black poodle. The man wore a bright pink shirt that read *Shampooches Dog Grooming* across the front. For a second, Genesis thought it was some kind of joke. That maybe Arthur had come up with another way to torment her for rejecting him, but no, this man was Yarrow Lupin, the Sowell Gate Pack Alpha.

They sat in a ramshackle outdoor theater space that was little more than a metal carport with a few pallets stacked to make a stage of sorts, a couple log benches sat upfront, but the rest of the seating was a mishmash of broken chairs and milk crates. Hardly a formal establishment. Her supposed grandmother's cave was more put together than this. The Sowell Gate Pack was looking more and more like a bunch of loosely banded rogues by the second.

"What brings you to Sowell Gate, Rogue?" Yarrow growled.

He didn't sound angry, per se, but definitely annoyed.

"I came searching for my parents. I was abandoned with a note warning me never to come here. Obviously, I didn't listen," she replied.

There was no use lying to the Alpha. Any hope she had of getting out of here without punishment for what she did to Arthur could only involve the absolute truth from her.

"Did you find them?"

"No, they're dead, but I reconnected with my grandmother."

"So, what's this about Arthur trying to force a claim on you? From his accounts, you two are already mated, and this male was the aggressor," Yarrow said.

"Yeah, so that's complicated. Arthur and I were tied together at birth by a warlock. My mother stole me away because she didn't believe in it. She let my father believe she had killed me instead of letting the promise be fulfilled. My father killed her because of it and then died himself for killing her. He died before the terms of the deal he made with Arthur's family were done, so technically, the binding was never complete. Arthur didn't take well to that, and when he saw I was happy with someone else, a non-Shifter, he attacked," Genesis knew it was a lot to wrap your head around.

Baron gripped her hand tightly while Yarrow called forward one of the men who retrieved her from the camp. Yarrow whispered into the man's ear before turning his attention back to Genesis.

"I'll need to confirm that this binding story is plausible, but continue. Why did Arthur attack? Who provoked who first?"

"I told you, he tried to claim me, and my grandmother stepped in to stop him. She said I had a choice in the matter and that he would have to court me properly. I guess he thought maybe he'd catch me alone at my camp that night, but Baron was there. We were heading off the mountain because of the snow when Arthur attacked in his animal form. He didn't go after me first, Arthur went after Baron, and I defended my mate. In that, I had every right to kill him, but I didn't. I showed mercy."

Yarrow scowled the entire time she spoke. He didn't speak for several minutes before turning his eyes to Baron.

"Did you know about Shifters before last night?"

Baron shook his head. "Fuck no, I'm still wrapping my head around all of this. Hell, this whole mate concept was something she sprung on me this morning."

Yarrow turned back to Genesis. "You marked him without explaining to him what that meant?" Now he was pissed, his Alpha energy rolling in waves, a prickly electric heat across her skin.

"There is no excuse for my actions, but I didn't mean to do it. My Bear was pissed and in full protection mode. I guess she thought it was the only way."

Yarrow held a hand up to stop her explanation. His gaze traveled over their shoulders to something or rather someone behind them. The man he had whispered to was now standing next to a tall, scowling woman. She stood with her arms crossed, exuding an energy that screamed 'don't fuck with me' and a little extra that made the hair on Genesis's arms stand on end. Genesis disliked whoever this woman was already.

"Artemis, we have a warlock situation," he said before explaining what Genesis had told him minutes earlier.

"Yikes, yeah, it's possible, and it's also true that if the terms of the deal aren't met, the binding isn't complete. Otherwise, she wouldn't have been able to refuse his claim. That kind of magic is banned for a reason. Does she still have the mark?" Artemis said.

"Mark? What mark?" Baron said, looking at Genesis.

Genesis sighed and pulled her shirt up, exposing her back. Artemis found the mark and traced it with a finger. "There is still a way for the deal to be completed. Otherwise, this mark would have died with her father. Her being already mated is a complication but not enough to override this. Do you know what the terms of the deal were? Maybe I can figure out a way to reverse the spell or counteract it," Artemis said.

"My grandmother said the deal was for Arthur's family to have my father reinstated into the Sowell Gate Pack, and when he became Alpha, he would ensure Arthur's family a permanent place of power within the Sowell Gate Pack," Genesis said.

Artemis pulled Genesis's shirt down. "Okay, so all you have to do is let her into the Pack and let her challenge you as Alpha. If she loses, the mark disappears, and she can go back to being rogue if she chooses," Artemis said.

Genesis gaped at the woman. "I have absolutely zero interest in being Alpha of anything. I'm not even an Alpha Shifter," she protested.

Artemis shrugged. "The alternative is days of excruciating blood rituals that could leave you both physically and mentally scarred for the rest of your life and still might not even work. Now, if we do it the way I suggest, not only will you be free of it by tomorrow night, but if you decide to stay Pack, your mate will also be Pack and provided protection from harm beyond your sole reach. Your choice."

Genesis bit her lip and looked at Baron before kissing him. "Even if you still want to end this, I can't leave you alone knowing you are unprotected," she said.

"I have zero clue what the hell is going on here, but Genesis, I'm here to protect you. Do what's best for you. Whatever this is between us can be sorted out later," he said.

Artemis snorted. "Look, human. You've been marked. Being physically marked in Shifter society is like an ironclad 'til death do you part contract. You heard the story of her parents. Her mother was human; she could run, but he couldn't. For Shifters, not being with one's mate is a death sentence. She should have thought it through, but obviously, that isn't a strong suit of her bloodline," Artemis said.

Genesis wanted to punch the snotty little witch, but she wasn't lying. If Genesis had known what it truly meant, she would have fought her Bear harder. Now it was too late.

Yarrow spoke up then. "Artemis, take Mr. Cross to the office, and you and Vega explain to him about the mating process. Rogue, follow me," Yarrow said.

"My name is Genesis," she said but stood to follow him, anyway.

"You're Rogue until you become Pack," he replied.

"So, how exactly does this work?"? she asked, ignoring his dismissive comment.

"Look, I believe you about Arthur. He and his family like having the prestige of power without all the stress, so it makes them convenient to delegate to. I, however, don't put it past them to have wanted to out the Alpha of the time for someone they could easily manipulate. Anyway, we'll make you official Pack. There isn't anything crazy to it, especially since you were born Pack. All you have to do is find your name in our log, sign as an adult, and pledge loyalty to the Pack in front of a few witnesses and me," Yarrow said, pointing to a massive tome spread on a large wooden desk.

"The humans who found me gave me the name Genesis. I don't know what I was called before then."

"Your grandmother never told you?"

"We didn't exactly get to that point."

"I was wondering about that, but given the melodrama and trickery, I'm guessing your grandmother is Betsy. The story of her son Gunnar is used as a cautionary tale for young children in the Pack. Which would make you, Ursa."

Genesis gasped before bursting into another fit of laughter. "You can't be serious?"

Yarrow scowled. "What, you don't like the name?"

"No, I mean. I use the name Ursa for my pen name."

Yarrow made another face, this time of disgust. "Don't tell me you're that romance author Gen Ursa," he nearly spat as he said the name.

Genesis stopped laughing and got defensive. "Oh god, don't tell me you're one of those romance isn't serious literature douchebags," she said.

Yarrow shook his head. "It ain't the romance I take offense to. It's all the made-up bullshit about Shifters. My mate is a huge fan of yours, by the way, which is the only reason your books are even on my radar. You're perpetuating some dangerous stereotypes, young lady," he said.

Genesis shrugged. "I guess that is a valid critique, but like I said, I grew up with humans. My only mentor was an old rogue who obviously didn't do a good job of teaching me the ropes. Anyway, it's fiction, not real life, and I doubt you'd appreciate me telling the world real Shifter secrets in my books either," she said.

Yarrow tilted his head to the side. "I guess not. At least this way, I don't have to get on you about outing Shifter business to the world. Just one request," he said.

"Yes, oh mighty Alpha," she said, quirking an eyebrow.

"Stop writing your Wolf Shifters as cowardly waifs. I know you're a Bear, so they gotta be the heroes in your story, but none of the Wolf Shifters you've met in this camp are anything like the ones in your books. Just saying, don't be such an animalist," he said.

"Wow, animalist? Is that a real thing? Well, I guess I can make an attempt, and by the way, all my Wolf Shifters are cowardly waifs because the only two I'd met before this trip were exactly that," she said.

Yarrow just grunted and flipped a few pages in the book until he found the entry of her birth. She hadn't been given a last name, just Ursa, so she signed her name Genesis Ursa Mabry.

"What, not taking the Cross name? I don't blame you. The Cross's have a long, turbulent history with the Native and Shifter communities here. The latest generation isn't as bad as their forefathers, but not by much. Can't say I'm excited to add a Cross to the ranks," Yarrow said.

"I can't say I'm a fan of the Cross family yet either, but Baron is different. I hope. As far as taking his name, it's too soon for that kind of talk. We may be mated by Shifter standards, but wedding bells are a long way off," she said.

Yarrow shook his head. "Well, your name is signed. Calix should have had enough time to gather up some witnesses for yours and Baron's induction ceremony. Baron will have to sign his name too, as your mate, and then tomorrow afternoon, if you're fully healed, we will have a brief challenge ceremony. I'm sorry that I can't go easy on you, but I'll not do any damage that will last more than a day or so. If you were an Alpha Shifter, we could skip the physical challenge, but since you aren't, there is no way you could best me in will," Yarrow said.

"Thank you?" Genesis said. She wasn't sure how to respond to that. Like, he was literally spelling out that he was obligated to kick her ass, and unless she wanted to become a mind slave to Arthur, Genesis would have to just deal. They left the book and found Baron waiting with Artemis and a few others.

Baron looked nervous like he was ready to run for the hills, but when she got closer, he pulled her into his arms and kissed her. "You don't have to do this for me. I appreciate it, I really do, but I don't want to be the reason you are stuck somewhere you don't want to be," he said softly.

Genesis smiled, tears in her eyes before she kissed him back. "Super cliché, but I want to be where you are. Even if we don't end up being each other's endgame, I would like to see where it goes with us. And for that to happen, I need to get Arthur literally and figuratively off my back," she said.

Baron nodded and then turned to Yarrow. "Can we get this over with? I need to have a private conversation with my mate," Baron said to Yarrow, which earned him a glare from just about everyone.

The ceremony was simple and plain, everyone wanting it to be done as quickly as possible. Genesis went first, kneeling before Yarrow and declaring her loyalty to the Pack and Yarrow as the Alpha of the Pack, and then it was Baron's turn. He didn't seem too excited about the whole ordeal, but Genesis held his hand through it, and then he signed his name next to hers in the Pack ledger.

"I'll see you back here at noon. Do not be late. Your ride is waiting at the end of the road," Yarrow said, dismissing them both.

Baron took Genesis's hand in his, and they walked the dirt road toward the highway together.

"I feel like I need to apologize again for all of this. I never meant to force you into any of this," she said.

"I appreciate the apology, but you aren't completely at fault for all of this. We were supposed to be a one-night thing. I forced myself into your plans, and not because I'm some awesome guy who just wanted to make sure you were safe, but because I wanted more time buried between your legs. So yeah, I played with a fucking Bear and got bit.

I'm responsible for my own actions that led us here, and I'm man enough to accept the consequences," he said.

"I don't want to be a consequence or an obligation."

"I don't either, but here we are. Romantic, ain't it?" he chuckled.

Genesis fought the urge to punch him. "Ugh, I guess I should just be satisfied that you don't hate me yet?"

"I don't hate you. I hate this situation. I'm not ready to make another long-term commitment, but if I was, I can't say committing to you would be a mistake," he said.

"I'm not asking for commitment here. I just hope that you'll want to date or something because I'd be lying if I said I could handle not having you between my legs every week," she said.

"Just every week?"

"Too much? Once a month then?"

"Fuck, woman, you think I could hold out a month after spending the last few days chasing your ass all over a mountain for a single moment of your time?"

"So, you don't just don't hate me. You like me?"

"Did we just transport back to middle school? Do I have to write you a little note and origami mail my intentions to you?"

Genesis laughed. "That would be cute," she said.

Baron paused before grabbing a stick from the ground and drawing out two check boxes with a Y and an N next to them before attempting a very poor *will you be my girlfriend?* in the soft dirt. Then he handed her the stick and stood back to watch. Genesis shook her head, moving the stick back and forth before Baron grabbed her hand and steered her to make an x in the box for yes.

"There, you happy?" he said and tossed the stick to the ground.

"I thought you didn't want to force me into anything," she said.

Baron gave her an incredulous stare before pulling his shirt to the side. His mark was no longer a huge wound; it was fully healed, and the puncture marks were concealed in an intricate tattoo of a snarling Brown Bear. "You keep playing like you don't want this but don't you forget, you were the one who literally bit my ass to stake your claim," he said.

Genesis closed the space between him and placed her hand over her mark, his eyes fluttered closed, and he groaned, not in pain but with arousal. "How did this get here?"

"That Artemis chick ain't so bad after all. She fixed me up and gave me a magic mark to make it less bite mark, more art."

"Did you choose the Bear, or did she?"

"I did, and look, it's my favorite color," he said.

Genesis couldn't help herself then, she stood on her tiptoes to kiss him, and he kissed her back. They got lost in each other until a familiar voice rang through the air.

"Y'all got me out here on the fucking highway worried as shit, and y'all are just necking like teenagers in the woods! Hurry y'all asses up. Aunt Melinda is waiting, and I, for one, do not want to be added to her shit list after this shit," Hunter said.

Baron pulled away and gave his cousin the finger but dragged Genesis along.

"Ugh, I have to meet your mother, now?"

"Oh, so I get inducted into a whole ass secret society, but you meeting my mom is too much?"

"Okay, okay, you have me there."

Chapter Nine

Baron wasn't excited at all for the showdown that would happen as soon as he got home. He spent most of the drive trying to formulate answers to all the questions his family would have, but he was now sworn not to answer truthfully. Genesis was no help. She spent the drive trading barbs with Hunter like it was the two of them who grew up together. She somehow knew just how far she could push him and what buttons to push without Baron having to step in. Maybe she would fit in with the Cross clan after all. Hunter was the easy one, to be honest, but most people had a hard enough time dealing with him.

"Look, I told y'all not to go get no bush wedding, and what do you do? Exactly that!" Hunter spat as they pulled up the drive to the main house.

"We aren't married, at least not legally. It was more a promise cere-mony," Baron tried. If he could get Hunter to buy that, then he might have a slim shot at selling it to the rest of the family. Artemis had explained that a Shifter mating was the same as a human marriage, just without the paperwork. Genesis's bite was as good as a ring on his finger as far as the supernatural community was concerned, and the fact that he'd just learned about Shifters meant he was still trying to figure out if this was all some elaborate joke or if he'd stepped through some alternate timeline on his flight home. All the same players, but now with a new light shone on the whole shebang.

"Nice try, man, but I ain't buying it. Might as well tell your Ma you went and got hitched 'cause there ain't no way in hell she's going to be okay with anything less than a declaration of love or a complete fucking psychotic break for your actions these last few days. Anyway, thanks for officially making Bechet the favorite son. Good luck living that shit down," Hunter said and got out of the car.

"I don't know if I love your cousin or hate him, but he is irritating as fuck," Genesis said.

Baron nodded in agreement. "We need to get our story straight before we go inside," he said.

"The best stories are the ones closest to the truth. We met, and things happened quickly for us in terms of emotional attachment, but we are going to take our time to see if things pan out. Simple, elegant. Not a lie," Genesis said and got out of the car.

Baron followed, slipping his arm around her waist as they entered the house. The whole family waited in the sitting room, looking like a country gothic painting. At least, the giant stuffed Bear that his father had shot to ease Bechet's fear after a strange encounter in the woods was no longer a prominent feature of the room. Now knowing the truth about Shifters in the mountains, he felt bad for teasing Bechet for falling for the family lore about why Cross men weren't welcome on the other side of the mountain. Thank god Braxton's son Brayden had thrown such a fit upon seeing the thing that his mother finally got the old man to move it to his office. At least, Genesis would never have a reason to ever go there.

"Baron, who is your lovely guest?" his mother asked.

Baron tried not to show an ounce of panic, even as sweat poured down his face. His mother was playing it cool, which meant she was anything but.

"Mother, family, meet my fiancée, Genesis Mabry."

Fuck, he'd fucked up. He was supposed to say friend, not fiancée. Girlfriend at the most. Even Genesis stiffened at his side before whipping around to face him.

"What happened to the plan?" she whispered.

"Sorry," he said and kissed her cheek.

Most of his family sat in stunned silence, but Hunter cackled like a hyena in the corner.

"I told you it was gonna be good. Hell, Baron didn't even last a half-second before failing under pressure. Boy, am I glad I'm not you, Baron. Sorry, Genesis. Welcome to the Cross family," he said and came over to give her a quick hug.

"Sorry, it's just a shock since it's so soon after Baron's divorce," Bechet said.

"You aren't sorry. Otherwise, you wouldn't have brought up Baron's divorce. Focus on yourself," Genesis snapped.

Isis stood, ready to get in Genesis's face, but Bechet held her back.

"Well, um, Brax and I are definitely excited that Baron has found someone who he obviously cares a lot about," Carmen said, shifting the giant baby in her arms from one hip to the other.

"Thank you," Baron finally unstuck his jaw.

He hadn't realized how much his relationship with his family had changed over the years. He'd thought he'd had his brothers' respect, that his parents trusted his judgment. Now he realized, how could they when he hadn't been able to trust his own damn self. He felt tears stinging the back of his eyes as he saw the very real concern his family had for his wellbeing, not in the oh-you-scared-us-this-once but more of an is-this-the-final-straw-before-we-send-you-on-a-long-spa-vacation.

Baron couldn't face them any longer. It was like a funhouse mirror reflecting all of his flaws and reckless behavior. The lump in his throat returned, and it felt like another larger one rested on his shoulders and chest. Genesis stopped glaring at his family and turned them both, so they were facing each other.

She held his gaze, concern clear in her eyes but not the same as his family's. She wasn't waiting for him to fall apart. She was there to steady him. To encourage him and give him strength. He knew then that he'd made the right choice. Genesis was the right choice for him. He matched her breathing, letting his body relax, not caring one bit that his family watched them. Watched as she helped him fight off the panic attack, instead of just letting it happen like they all had for years.

He turned to face his family with a new resolve. "I don't care if you approve of my relationship with Genesis or not. I'm letting you know as a courtesy because you are my family, and I love you, and I want to share the good parts of my life with you, even if you choose to only see the bad," he said, directing his last comment at Bechet.

Surprisingly, it was his father, Wilhelm, who spoke first. "Look, son, you can't blame us for being a little wary about some girl you only just met, but as long as she ain't trapping you with a baby and having you run off and get married by a hippie, I'm good with whatever decision you make," Wilhelm said.

"Carmen didn't trap me with a baby. I trapped her, and Yarrow Lupin is a registered officiant, not a hippie or a shaman like Hunter likes to say," Braxton said.

"Pretty sure the baby comment was about Christine, but if the shoe fits," Hunter chuckled, earning him a glare from just about everyone.

"What? Too soon? Baron's obviously moved on to greener pastures, so sue me," he said.

"Just when you were getting to be my favorite," Genesis said.

"Hunter? The favorite in-law? You just haven't spent time with the rest of us, but with you two engaged, I'm sure that's going to be changing real soon," Braxton said.

"Exactly, so when shall we expect the truck with your things?" Baron's mother asked.

Baron started to panic again. They hadn't exactly talked about that yet; if she would stay with him, where she had even lived prior to this trip. Baron had no idea.

"Actually, I'll be staying in Sowell City. I have some unfinished business there that I need to wrap up, and after that, we'll make the decision on if I move in with Baron, or he moves in with me," Genesis said.

"Oh, this is going to be good," Hunter said, rubbing his hands together with anticipation.

"Wait, not living here is an option?" Carmen said, glaring at Braxton.

"See what you started," Braxton glared at Baron.

"Because of my job, our legal residence has to be in Mulberry, but we split our time between there and here," Isis said.

"We live here full time but keep a place in Sowell for when Carmen has work engagements that don't allow for her to safely travel the two hours between here and the city for her job to get done," Braxton said.

"So, what is it that you do, Genesis? It seems my son is at a loss for pertinent information about you and your plans," his mother asked.

"I just finished college last year with a degree in journalism and business management. Writing romance novels is my passion, but freelance pieces and my travel blog help pay the bills. I also love the outdoors, and you won't catch me inside unless I'm on deadline or the weather is bad," Genesis said.

"Wait, how old are you?" Hunter asked.

"I don't think that's an appropriate question," Baron said.

"You're just afraid you picked up an underaged girl," Hunter replied.

"I paid for college myself, and I didn't want loans, so I'm older than you think," Genesis offered, and that was all she was going to offer.

"Well, at least she's educated," his mother said.

"And not afraid of hard work," Wilhelm Cross added.

Baron felt like dying from embarrassment. His family truly was a mess. He knew things were going to get worse the longer they stayed, so he grabbed Genesis's hand and started pulling her toward the door.

"It's been a long day. We'll see you all at breakfast," he called over his shoulder as he dragged Genesis out of the house.

She started giggling as soon as they were outside. "Wow, that was not what I expected," she said.

"That bad?" He winced.

"Nah, I grew up in the foster system before being adopted by the Mabrys at ten. I've seen plenty of crazy family drama. Your family is rude and quirky, a little bougie, but I can tell you guys are genuinely caring," she said.

"You can tell that from five minutes?"

Genesis shrugged. "I had to learn how to read people. Call it a survival skill."

Baron pulled her into his arms and kissed her. "Life is about more than just surviving. You've got to find some time to actually live," he said.

Genesis kissed him back.

"Well, I'm about to live the next hour in that massive tub of yours, so let's go, lumberjack," she said and took off running toward his house.

Shaking his head, Baron chased after her.

Breakfast with Baron's family went a lot better than their first meeting. Genesis had fun chatting about hiking trails with Carmen. Isis was cordial, but they didn't have much in common to keep any real conversation going, especially with Isis making sure to say "off the record" every few sentences, before Genesis decided it was better to just avoid talking to her as much as possible. She had a degree in journalism, sure, but politics and gossip had never been her thing. She didn't blame Isis for being on guard, she was a politician, but it was clear her icy attitude was built in.

"Don't worry about Isis. She will warm up to you eventually," Carmen said after rescuing her from another one of Isis's prepared talking points.

Genesis could only take the woman's word for it. "So, how does it work? You living here and taking care of your son while also working in Sowell. That's a rough drive to make on a daily basis," Genesis said.

Carmen rolled her eyes. "It is, but I don't do it daily. I've had to modify the hours at my studio to three days a week and every other weekend. It's a lot, but Brax and our son are worth it," she said, smiling at her husband from across the room.

"One day, you'll have to tell me your story. I'm a sucker for true love," Genesis said.

"Well, our story was a whole lot of fucking before feelings. Anyway, you said you write romance. Do you publish, or do you just do it for fun? What sub-genre?"

Carmen's question was just loud enough to garner the attention of the whole group. Genesis did not like to be put on the spot. She used a pen name for a reason.

"I see you are a romance reader," Genesis laughed.

"She sure is. Her friend Amayah got her hooked on these ridiculous WereBear novels. I mean, the sex scenes are good inspiration, but the rest of it is a bunch of hogwash," Braxton said.

Genesis was used to the major gap between her fans and her detractors, but she was still a little taken aback that anyone in Baron's family read her books, let alone were fans. Even if begrudgingly.

"Oh, so you read them too?" Hunter laughed.

"A real man strives to know his wife's interests. Besides, you think I was gonna let her walk around with half-naked men on her books and not see what it was all about?" Braxton replied.

Genesis was glad the spotlight wasn't on her any longer as the family began discussing romance novels from a male and female perspective. Wilhelm surprised them all by saying he'd used a romance novel as a guidebook to woo his wife, Melinda. Braxton admitted that he, too, had turned to his limited knowledge of romance novels in his plan to make Carmen see him as more than a fling.

The conversation lasted longer than Genesis expected, and soon Baron was pulling her out of her chair and marching her toward the door.

"Sorry to eat and run, but we have some business in Sowell today," Baron said, guiding her out the door.

"Is it that time already?" Genesis groaned.

"Yeah, unfortunately," Baron muttered as they climbed into his truck.

Genesis couldn't believe it had only been a week since she'd first climbed into the primer blue relic. Baron held her hand the entire drive over the mountain and out to Sullah.

"You don't have to stay for the challenge. I know it might be hard for you to watch me fight," Genesis said.

Baron squeezed her hand tighter. "Yeah, it's going to be rough, but I'm not leaving your side. I know you aren't planning to win this thing, but I'll be rooting for you just the same," he said.

"At least, the fight will be quick. I'll have to fight back for the first few minutes, but then I'll submit, and this will all be over," Genesis said.

"Brax gave me the keys to his and Carmen's place for the night, so we won't have to return right away," Baron said.

Genesis didn't know that was even an issue for her until Baron mentioned it. "Thank you," she said, fighting back tears.

"I may not have much to offer you, Genesis. Especially not in this situation, but know that I've got your back. Whatever happens."

Baron raised her hand up to press a kiss to the back of her hand. The effect of his sweet words, combined with the warmth of his lips, worked its way through her, calming her nerves.

Baron gripped the wooden bench so tight he could hear the wood splintering beneath his grip. He'd known he would get riled up seeing Genesis fight, but he had no idea just how brutal the fight would actually be. Genesis's Bear had held her own for the first five minutes, using her size to dominate the beginning of the fight, but Yarrow's Wolf was faster and more vicious. It knew just when and where to strike for maximum effect.

Baron clenched his teeth when the Wolf caught Genesis's Bear in the leg, tearing a hole in it large enough to incapacitate her. She fell to the ground with a roar. Now in a kneeling position, Genesis lowered her head while the Wolf paced around her. It growled low and menacing, snapping at Genesis every time a muscle even twitched in her body. Then she shifted back to human form. Most of her wounds healed in the transition, but there were plenty of bruises and bites that left little rivulets of blood pouring down her arms and legs.

"I revoke my challenge. I submit to your will as Alpha," Genesis said.

The Wolf stopped right in front of Genesis and shifted back into Yarrow's massive frame.

"This challenge is done. Genesis Ursa Mabry has submitted with honor and will return to the Pack in her rightfully earned position as Beta of Sowell Gate Pack," Yarrow said.

There was a murmur in the crowd. Baron frowned. He had no idea what that even meant. Even Genesis looked shocked and confused by Yarrow's proclamation. The enforcers from the camp moved forward, along with Artemis. Artemis touched Genesis between the shoulder blades, her hand glowing the same eerie green it had when she'd cast the spell to heal and change Baron's own mark.

Genesis winced and bit her lip as a thick plume of smoke rose from her skin.

Then Artemis stepped back. "The mark is gone. You're no longer beholden to the bond," she said before leaving the circle.

The asshole enforcer, who Baron had come to learn was Yarrow's own brother Calix Lupin, grabbed Genesis by the arm and lifted her to standing before positioning her next to Yarrow. He moved back to the group of enforcers, and all four men knelt before Yarrow and Genesis.

"The Pleasure Pack is at your service, under the command of the Alpha."

Baron scowled. The only Pleasure Pack Genesis would ever need was permanently attached to him. He started to make a move, but the woman next to him put a hand on his shoulder.

"Don't mind the title. It's some made-up bullshit they've used since they were kids. All they mean is that they recognize her status above them in the Pack hierarchy," the older woman said.

"Genesis is now the second in command?"

"Pretty much. Arthur was holding the position in an acting capacity, but after he attacked you and lied to the Alpha, he was removed. Since Genesis bested Arthur in the fight and conducted herself with honor in this challenge to Yarrow, he's rewarding her with the position."

"She has no say in this?"

"Genesis can decline the position, but I hope she doesn't. It's been a long time since this Pack had a proper hierarchy, and it'd be nice to see it back to its true glory," the woman said.

There was a bit more ceremony involved, and Baron found himself sticking by the older woman's side since she seemed willing to help explain it all to him.

"When are you and my granddaughter going to get a proper binding ceremony?" the woman asked as things began to wind down.

Baron turned wide-eyed at the more petite woman. "You're Genesis's grandmother?"

"The name's Betsy. Answer the question, son," she said.

"We're following the human customs in our relationship. Treating the mating as an engagement," Baron said.

The woman tsked and pinched his arm hard. "You humans don't understand nothing. As far as I'm concerned, you are already married. However, with Genesis's new standing in the Pack, y'all gotta set the example for these young kids. Mating a human doesn't mean trashing the Shifter way of things," she said.

"That isn't our intent, I assure you," Baron said.

"Good, so get on with it. I'll expect to hear about a date within the next few weeks," Betsy said and walked away.

Baron stared after the woman in shock. "Hey! You ready to go?" Genesis said, coming up beside him.

Baron turned to look at her. She was fully dressed now and patched up with a few bandages. "I just met your grandmother," he said.

Genesis scowled. "Betsy—not sure I'm ready to call her grandma yet. Don't mind her. I want to get someplace comfortable before we talk about what just happened and what that means going forward," Genesis said.

Genesis started to walk away, but she had a pronounced limp that Baron did not like. He grabbed her and cradled her in his arms as he marched back to his truck.

"I can walk, you know?" Genesis laughed.

"Sure, you can, but this is better," Baron said.

Back on the estate, Genesis convinced Baron to give her some time alone in the woods so she could shift again and heal.

"I've gotta check in with my family again, but it shouldn't take me long. I'll meet you back at the house."

Genesis nodded and hobbled further into the brush. Baron, ever the gentleman, had helped her to walk into the tree line. He probably would have carried her if she had allowed it. Feeling the burning in her leg, Genesis regretted that decision a little. Despite the forest being warm enough for the thickest of the snow to have melted away, there was still a thin layer of frost on the ground. It would be way too easy for her to slip up and hurt herself even worse.

I'm waiting.

Just a little farther to make sure no one can accidentally happen upon us.

The Bear was getting impatient, but Genesis held her firm. She needed to shift in order to heal quicker. Genesis had no plans of letting the Bear roam. She had a date with her mate that she refused to be late for. When Genesis was ready, she opened the way for her Bear to rush forward. The cracking dismemberment of her joints was more evident because of her injuries, but once fused back together, she was completely healed, although in her Bear form. The once gray forest was now vibrant with smells and textures. She could taste the lingering ice in the air and smell the decaying leaves buried under snow. Hear the creatures of the forest as they scurried about.

The Bear took a few steps toward the wild wilderness, the siren's call of Sowell Gate's energy beckoning her, but Genesis forced herself back into human form before the Bear got too far in.

Run!

But what about our mate?

The Bear remained quiet inside of her, so Genesis took that as a begrudging agreement that time with Baron was more important at that moment. She headed back to the cabin and let herself in. Baron hadn't locked the door when they had left and hadn't mentioned her needing a key to get in. Baron was nowhere in sight, but on the kitchen counter was a mason jar full of a dark purple substance with a bow tied around it. Curious, Genesis picked it up and smiled. It was labeled Mirna's Special Jam. Feeling a bit hungry after all the running, Genesis decided to make herself some toast to sample some of this special concoction.

While she waited for her toast to finish, she scooped up a tiny spoonful and gave it a sniff. It smelled simple enough. Like sugar and wild berries, but when she flicked her tongue over the sticky jam, she moaned out loud, "Holy fuck, that's good!"

She savored the rest of the spoonful before forcing herself to close the jar. If she wasn't careful, she might finish the whole thing before being able to share with Baron, its intended recipient. Thankfully, she could already hear his heavy footfalls trudging up the stairs out front.

"Sorry that took so long. Did you and your Bear have a good walk?" Baron said, shrugging out of his jacket.

"Yeah, but it was a short one. I wanted to get back to you and couldn't trust that she wouldn't take off for longer than I can safely allow," Genesis admitted.

It was nice being able to speak so openly about her Bear and its needs.

Baron nodded. "Understandable, but won't it be worse if you don't let her run? Maybe I can come with you to help with keeping her close by."

Genesis shook her head. "That's too dangerous. I can shift for a few minutes in the bathroom so she can shake out her fur, and then tomorrow go on a nice long run."

"You sure she won't wreck the place?"

"No, but I'm hoping she knows better. It's not like this is the first time. It's just she's gotten so used to her freedom out here, and Sowell Gate is like a magnet to her."

"Well, if you do need to go for a longer run, just let me know so I won't worry. I wouldn't want her to feel uncomfortable here any more than I want you to," Baron said, taking Genesis into his arms.

Genesis cuddled into him. "Oh, we are both quite comfortable here with you."

He rubbed her back gently before his hands slid under the hem of her shirt. The instant his skin came in contact with hers, the mood shifted from one of communal exhaustion to one of intense sexual tension. Genesis reached between them and began to unbutton the flannel shirt he wore, trailing soft kisses along each new piece of skin she revealed. Baron hissed, and his touch became more urgent and needy as he gripped and massaged her.

"I thought you were exhausted," he managed after a moment.

"Mmm, exhausted but horny. So very, very horny," she sighed between kisses.

"Is that right?" He pulled her shirt over her head, temporarily halting her mouth's exploration of his broad chest and toned abdomen.

As soon as her hands were free, Genesis shimmied out of her pants. Once completely naked, she kept her distance even as he reached for her. "Bed or couch?"

Baron made quick work of his jeans and boxers. His rigid staff bobbed in the space between them. Genesis licked her lips but made no move to touch him. They stood there for several minutes, drinking in each other's bodies.

"Have I ever told you how beautiful you are?"

"Not in so many words but definitely in how you respond to me," Genesis said.

"That's a shame. I should have said it a million times. You're beautiful, Genesis. So fucking beautiful, and you're all mine," he growled at the end of the sentence, and his long stride closed the minimal distance between them. His lips met hers before he lifted her up and impaled her on his massive cock.

"I guess the answer was neither," she gasped as she held on tight to his shoulders. His hips bucked wildly as he leaned against the door to steady himself. Genesis enjoyed every minute of the wild ride he was giving her, especially as he tore his mouth from hers and latched on to her breast.

"Baron," she cried out as her first orgasm tore through her body.

Her cry only earned her a more vigorous fucking, and she was glad she'd taken the time to heal fully before initiating this coupling with her mate; otherwise, she wouldn't have been able to enjoy it half as much as she was.

"Tell me if it's too much," Baron gasped as if reading her mind.

"No, fuck. It's perfect. Your perfect."

More!

Genesis chuckled at her Bear's agreement just before another orgasm began to creep its way into her system. She bucked her hips, desperate to keep pace with him, even as her body slipped into sensory overload. At this rate, she might not even be able to enjoy her orgasm before she lost consciousness. She dropped her head to his shoulder and nipped at his mating mark. Just as it threatened to overcome her, Baron slammed into her, his thick member pulsing with his release. His ragged breath dragged along her sweat-slicked skin as they both rode out the waves of their passion.

Baron nearly collapsed as his knees gave way. Yet, he had just enough strength to guide them both gently to the floor. "Holy fuck, what kind of shifter magic did you just do?"

"That good?" Genesis laughed.

He wrapped his arms tight around her and pulled her on top of him. "I came so hard it might take me a week to recover."

Genesis looked between their bodies and shook her head. "Nope, you're still hard."

Baron followed her gaze and shook his head. "Shit! Then let's move this to the bed. I want to do that again."

CHAPTER TEN

Genesis burst into Baron's office with a huge grin on her face. "You won't believe the call I just got!"

Baron looked up from the computer screen where he'd been taking the online practice exam for state employment. He noted the mischievous glint in her eyes and sat back in his chair. This was a new expression for him to see. Not that he hadn't seen it before, but this time was different because, for the first time, it wasn't right before she'd said something naughty to him that would eventually lead to them fucking.

Genesis rounded his desk, and he pulled her into his lap. "That you just won the lottery and want to fuck on a giant pile of cash?"

She shook her head. "I like where your thoughts are going but gross. Do you know how filthy money is? Anyway, we'll discuss this fantasy of yours more at a later date. My call actually has something to do with Hunter."

Baron scowled. "I'm sorry, but I thought we agreed I don't share."

"Oh stop, that isn't even close. I just need you to clear Florian Falconer to come to the Estate so I can train with him here instead of all the way in Sullah."

"Oh, is that all? What does that have to do with Hunter?"

"Come on, you were the one who told me about their little love triangle. Maybe I can use a little of my romance knowledge to help them mend whatever is keeping them apart. I mean, we both saw the sparks, right? No way that's a done deal between them."

"I don't want you messing with my cousin's personal life, but I will allow Florian access to the Estate. Only because if he trains you here, I have more time with you."

Genesis kissed him on each cheek and then on his lips. Only he didn't allow her to get away with a simple peck of the lips. He caught her bottom lip between his teeth, nipping it before sucking her lip into his mouth. She moaned and swept her tongue into play for a moment before she pulled away.

"Save that for tonight. Anyway, that isn't my only news."

"No?"

"I need to handle a few things back home before I can stay for good."

"Okay, that isn't a problem."

"So, you're okay with me going for a few days?"

Baron sighed and cupped her chin in his hand. "Listen, I know we are mated, and even though I'm still wrapping my head around what all that means, it doesn't mean I aim to control you or limit you in any way. As long as we are open and honest with each other."

"Alright, I was thinking I could go this weekend. Get things settled before I get too far into things with being the new Beta, and it's harder to go."

"This weekend? Did you want me to come with you?" Baron had to ask because he wanted to be there to support her if needed. Well, maybe just to be with her in general, but he hoped she would ask him to go with her, anyway. He was curious to see the final piece to the Genesis puzzle. Her life before him.

In the last month, they'd both been busy adjusting to their new reality. He'd admitted to himself that taking over as Head of Cross Logging wasn't what he wanted to do in life. Thankfully, Genesis was super encouraging of his choice to pursue his dream of being a Park Ranger. He was still gaining the courage to tell his family, but he figured that could wait until he passed the state exam.

Pack life had its own obligations, not to mention adjusting to living together with Genesis and her Bear. He'd be lying if he said things had been perfect every minute of every day, but whatever hiccups they encountered had only made them grow stronger as a couple and in their understanding of one another. It hurt when she pulled away from him and shook her head.

"This is something I need to do alone."

Baron leaned in and kissed Genesis. He didn't like her insistence on shutting him out of that part of her, but things between them were still new. He was willing to give her more time to adjust to the absolute honesty he demanded from her, and he too needed to extend a little more trust. Genesis was not Christine. "Then I will definitely be anxiously waiting for your return."

Genesis melted into him, and they got caught up in each other for a few moments, only breaking apart when the warning tone of his computer snapped them out of their love-filled haze.

"Oh! You're taking the test! You should have told me; I would have come later or told you over dinner," Genesis said, standing up.

"No, you and your news are way more important."

"It's a timed test, Baron. I know you've been really looking into becoming a park ranger, and I don't want to stand in the way of your dream," she admonished.

"You aren't. Besides, this is just a practice test. The real one is in person. Which I will take next month."

Genesis relaxed then and sank back into his lap. "Well then, if that's the case. Where were we?"

"Go lock the door."

"Are you sure you don't want me to come with you?" Baron asked.

Genesis wrapped her arms around her massive mate and kissed his cheek. "I believe you have applications to fill out," she replied.

Baron scowled. "They're online and will take maybe an hour. You are leaving me for three whole days to go back to your home base; one you still haven't revealed the location of to me," Baron said.

"What? Are you afraid I'll run away and never come back? Did you not pay attention during the intro to being a Shifter mate? I promise you if I'm gone longer than three days without so much as a phone call to hear your voice, I'm no longer of the living," Genesis said.

It was meant to be reassurance, but the way Baron's grip tightened around her waist told her she had maybe gone a bit too far. She knew she was asking a lot from him, and he'd been so easily persuaded when she'd first brought up the trip earlier that week. Yet, it was her fault for expecting him not to have further questions about her trip as the days passed.

"Fuck, I hate not knowing if these feelings I have for you are real or just some magical attachment," he said, his conflict in his eyes clear.

"I wish I had more answers for you about that, but isn't that why we are taking things slow? I mean, slowish."

"Let me come with you. Show me who Genesis really is, where you grew up. Who your friends are."

Genesis pulled out of his grasp and finished closing her backpack. "You still driving me to the airport?"

"Of course," Baron said and snatched her backpack off the bed before storming out of the room.

Genesis followed Baron to his truck and climbed into the passenger seat. They didn't speak again until they had cleared the mountain pass.

"You don't have to be ashamed of your past," Baron said.

"I'm not."

"Then why don't you talk about it? I've bared my soul to you, and all I know about you is that you can turn into a Bear and you write romance novels," Baron said.

"That's a hell of a lot, my dear Baron," Genesis snorted.

She watched as his grip tightened on the wheel. She didn't want him to be angry. It wasn't even like she thought it weird that he would be. Hell, if the situation were turned around, Genesis would be pissed too. The problem was Genesis didn't have much practice with showing all of herself to anyone.

The closest person to her was her foster brother, and even he didn't know everything. As it was, she'd have one hell of a time explaining to everyone what was going on. That was why she wanted to go alone. She didn't need Baron there to complicate things. To push her to reveal too much, too soon. If life had taught her anything, it was to keep things close to her chest and to never reveal her hand until absolutely necessary. Granted, that wasn't at all how things had happened with Baron, but that didn't mean she'd let one outlier in her experience change her whole outlook on life.

"At least, tell me you aren't hiding some boyfriend back home," he ground out.

Genesis sighed. "If there was someone serious, I never would have seduced you in the hotel room."

"I think I was the one who seduced you that night," Baron said.

"True, but I wouldn't have allowed things to go that far if I had been serious with someone."

"Alright, then why aren't you letting me help you with this move?"

"Because I'm used to handling things on my own, and having you there will complicate things and distract me," Genesis said.

"Finally, some truth! So why would I be a complication?"

"Because I'll have to explain. I won't be able to make a clean break," Genesis said.

"So, you don't want those closest to you to know about me," Baron said.

"I will tell those who are closest to me. Just not right now when I'm still trying to figure out what this is all really going to mean for me. I can't tell them about you without them getting suspicious about everything else. I've managed to keep my Shifter stuff to myself for so long. I'm not ready to risk them finding out now."

"I get it a little, but you were perfectly fine with dragging my family and me into a dangerous new world, but I can't be part of the one that made you who you are?"

"You can be angry all you want, but it's not going to change my decision. I'm not hiding you, Baron, but there are things in my life that I'd rather keep you out of. My supernatural genetics are nothing in comparison."

Genesis watched as Baron warred with himself. Vacillating between anger and concern. "Are you part of something illegal? Is it drugs? Is that why you travel so much?"

"Wow, seriously, Baron. That's what you think of me?"

"I don't know what to think, Genesis. You won't be honest with me, even knowing how much I need that from you."

"I am being honest with you. I don't want you to come. I can't be away from you or the Pack for that long. The details of my trip aren't important. The only thing that matters is that when I come back, I'll be here with you for good," she said.

Her answer wouldn't satisfy Baron, she already knew that, but she'd given him all she could at this point.

Baron was pissed. He was angry and hurt, and Genesis didn't seem to care one bit that she was the cause of it. For the first time since they'd met, Baron felt the need to withdraw from her. Well, maybe not the first time. He'd definitely had similar thoughts when she'd revealed herself as a Bear Shifter, but in his weakened and traumatized state, the thought had been fleeting.

He worked his jaw to keep from saying anything to continue the argument they were having. It was clear he couldn't change her mind, and if he insisted on following, it would only make him look like the asshole. He dropped her off at the airport with only a kiss and a half-hearted wave. Genesis didn't show a single moment of concern at his chaste goodbye. She just smiled and took off into the building without glancing back. Baron fought the urge to chase her down and kiss her properly, to make sure she knew he would be waiting for her return.

He got back in his SUV and headed back home. The farther he got away from the airport and Genesis, the more his heart ached, and his shoulder where her mark lay began to burn. The ache became so bad that Baron ended up making a detour to Braxton and Carmen's house in the city.

"You don't look so hot," Braxton said with a scowl when he opened the door for Baron.

"Genesis is gone," Baron said.

Braxton's eyes bugged before he moved out the way to let Baron inside.

"What do you mean she's gone? I thought you two were going to get her stuff," Braxton said.

Baron flopped down on Braxton's couch just as Carmen came out of the back with her camera bag on one shoulder and little Brayden on her hip.

"Oh! Hey Baron, I thought you would be on the plane with Genesis by now," Carmen said.

"She went without me," Baron said.

The verbal reminder sent another jolt of pain through his mating mark, and he winced. Something was wrong. The mating mark wasn't supposed to hurt like this.

"Oh," Carmen said, giving Baron a concerned look.

"Love, we're going to have some brother time. Why don't you go ahead to work?" Braxton said.

Carmen looked Baron over one more time before handing Brayden off to Braxton and kissing his cheek.

"Let me know if you two need anything," Carmen said.

"We'll be fine, love," Braxton assured his wife.

As soon as Carmen was gone, Braxton turned his concern back on Baron. The move made him sink further into the couch. He didn't want his family to be worried about him again. They had just started treating him without kid gloves. The last thing he needed was for them to think he was breaking again, and especially over a woman.

"So, tell me what happened," Braxton said.

"She wouldn't tell me where she was going, then she told me I couldn't come because it would make things complicated for her."

"Complicated how?"

"Exactly what I wanted to know. Anyway, we went back and forth the whole ride to the airport," Baron said.

"I'm guessing you look and probably feel like shit because you let your woman leave angry with you. You think she might not come back?" Braxton said.

"Yeah, and I have no way of contacting her besides her phone number," Baron said.

"Then call her. Is she on the plane yet?"

Baron shook his head. "I have no idea. She didn't share her itinerary with me, and I didn't push."

"You should have. Geez, I get things went fast for you two. Faster even than Carmen and me, but damn if you don't start acting like a man in love. You talked her into sending you her coordinates when you two were just strangers. Now that you're engaged, you can't even get her to share her flight details?"

"To be fair, the engagement was a slip of the tongue."

"That she went along with and is still going along with a month later. That sounds official enough for me. Call her. Leave her a voicemail if she doesn't answer. Trust me, you don't want her landing wherever she lands and not have any communication from you."

"I don't know if I can talk to her right now and not come off as an angry, insecure jerk," Baron said as he pulled out his phone.

"If the options are that or possibly not seeing her again, which one can you live with?"

Baron knew what his answer was, but he still hesitated. Braxton was just about to snatch his phone away when Genesis's number came up on his screen. She was calling him. The pain in his shoulder immediately eased when he heard her voice.

"I don't have much time to talk. I've already boarded. I just didn't want to leave things between us so volatile," she said.

"I just want to know more about you."

"I know, and when I get back, I'll tell you everything. I promise. I just need to do this on my own," Genesis said.

"I guess that will have to be enough for now," Baron said.

"I'm sorry, Baron. I have to go. I'll call when I land," Genesis said and hung up.

Braxton had moved to the kitchen to give Baron some privacy with his phone call, but it was clear he was watching him closely.

"Everything alright?" Braxton asked, coming back to the couch and handing Baron a beer.

Baron took a swig of the cool liquid before shaking his head. "Better but damn sure not as okay as it could be," he said.

"She's really leaving?"

"She'll be back. If not for me, for other things," Baron said.

"Then maybe you should make sure that when she does get back, you have something special waiting for her. Like maybe a proper engagement. I can see if Carmen's friends can help out with setting up something special, and if you don't want to go with a traditional ring, I can hook you up with my buddy who did Carmen's ring for me," Braxton offered.

"That won't be necessary. Like I said, the engagement is complicated. I feel like if I made a big deal about it right when she gets back, she might not enjoy that," Baron said.

"Dude, she's a romance author. How could a grand romantic gesture not be her thing? Just look up her books and see what she writes about. That will tell you all you need to know about what she likes and doesn't like in a relationship," Braxton said.

Baron laughed. "I don't even know her pen name. I've googled Genesis Mabry, and nothing has come up about her books, only her freelance articles and travel blog."

"Alright, well, did she give you any hints about what she writes? Ever look over her shoulder while she's working?"

Baron sat thinking for a moment. Genesis only seemed to work when he was busy with his own work. Baron also wasn't so nosy that he would peek over her shoulder the few times she'd been writing around him. Then he remembered a phone conversation he'd partially overheard. They had been about to share a shower together when she got the call. He left her to it, but the conversation had lasted longer than his solo shower. He hadn't heard much except that Genesis would need an extension on her latest draft.

"Do you think we could look it up based on character names?"

Braxton made a face. "Maybe, but it's a long shot if the names are too common."

"I don't think that will be a problem. How many people do you think are named Ragnar and Organza?"

Baron watched as his brother's concerned face turned to one of shock. Then he marched over to the bookshelf in the corner and pulled out one of Carmen's romance novels. Shaking his head, he dropped the book in Baron's lap.

"If I'm right about this, there is a reason she's so secretive about her writing. Gen Ursa's real identity is like the holy grail to her fans," Braxton said.

Baron picked up the novel and opened it to the back, where he found the author's bio. There was nothing to give away any personal information. Just that Gen Ursa was apparently a bawdy wood nymph, who traveled the world's forest lands collecting tales of romance to share with the world. A curvaceous Black fairy was drawn where her real picture would have gone; like Tinkerbell, but hotter. Baron shook his head as he scanned the book further. Sure enough, there was a teaser for the next book, touting the scandalous romance between Bear Shifter Ragnar and quirky seamstress Organza.

"Well, that's one mystery solved," he muttered.

"You should be stoked! I don't know how much romance authors make, but with the popularity and cult following of her work, she probably isn't one of those struggling writer types. Anyway, I can't wait to tell Carmen this. She's going to be so excited!"

Baron scowled at his brother. "You're not telling Carmen about this. You're not to tell anyone. We don't know for sure that Genesis is Gen Ursa. And even if we did, it's her thing to tell."

Braxton shrugged. "I can't make any promises I won't share my theory with Carmen. We have a strict no withholding policy."

"Fine, but try not to share your theory with anyone else."

"Alright, alright, grumpy. You got any plans to do something other than sulk on my couch all day?"

Baron sighed. In truth, he did have things to do. There was always more paperwork for him at the office and a few other things to do around the house that he'd neglected with Genesis around. Then again, Baron rarely got to hang out on this side of Sowell Gate. Maybe he should take the day and get to know Sowell City the way his brother and cousin had. So much had changed since his young and reckless days before his marriage. Just the thought of Christine left a bitter taste in his mouth. He may be over her, but he still had work to do when it came to getting over the damage left in her wake.

"Actually, I do. Mind if I take this with me?" Baron said, holding up the book.

Braxton snatched the book from his hand and returned it to the shelf before pulling out another much more worn book. "Take this one, and when you're done, you are welcome to come back for the next in the series."

Baron looked at the half-naked man on the cover, draped in a Bear pelt, and snorted. Knowing what he did now about the supernatural community, Baron had a feeling Gen Ursa kept her identity a secret for much bigger reasons than being the run-of-the-mill introvert author. The Shifter community would be pissed about the cover alone.

He tucked the book into his pocket and patted his nephew on the head before heading out the front door. "See you at dinner Sunday," he called over his shoulder.

"Enjoy the book," Braxton snickered.

Chapter Eleven

Genesis closed her eyes and took a deep breath. She held it for a count of four before letting it all out and pasting a smile on her face. There was no more stalling. She'd gotten into the city late and booked a hotel after chickening out about returning to her apartment with Victor. Then she decided it was only fair for her parents to know about her new relationship and move before he did.

She also hadn't wanted him to know she was leaving until the very last minute. No chasing her down to her adoptive parents' home or giving any extra time to cause a fuss. If she timed everything perfectly, she wouldn't have to speak to him at all. Her relationship with Victor was complicated and long overdue for an end, but that wasn't her biggest worry at the moment.

She pushed open the front door of the Mabry's and was instantly greeted by the couple's three yappy Yorkies, then was quickly engulfed in a hug by the Mabry's youngest biological son. The scent of an unwashed teen male assaulted her senses, and she was forced to hold her breath again as she wiggled out of his grasp.

"Oh my god! When did you last shower?" she gasped, finally getting enough space between her and him to breathe.

Gordan laughed and rubbed the top of her head like she was the younger sibling and not the other way around.

"Long time no see, shorty. What did you bring me?"

Genesis shook her head and pulled a Sowell City shot glass out of her purse and handed it to him. Gordon had quickly overshot her height by the time he was in middle school. How could he not when both his parents were Amazonian in size, Griffin being a solid 6'5" and Martha a willowy 5'10". Gordon was set to outgrow them all. Griffin being a wheelchair user after his accident, was the only reason anything in the house was appropriately within her reach.

"Genesis! What did we say about encouraging your brother's inappropriate collections?" Martha Mabry came strolling out of her office. Her long blonde hair was now cut into a neat pixie cut that showed off the slim, angular quality of her face and graceful neckline. As usual, she was dressed casual yet neat as a pin, beige cardigan over a white linen jumpsuit. Along with her signature pearls and carefully made-up no-makeup look.

"The dogs always shredded my postcards, and shot glasses can be found literally everywhere," Genesis offered as a halfhearted excuse.

"Come on, Mom. It's not like I'm actually using them," Gordan whined.

"You better not be," Martha snapped at him before crossing the foyer to give Genesis a hug. It was brief and almost chaste, but Genesis knew not to take offense. Martha wasn't an affectionate person in general.

"Where's Dad and the baby brat?" Genesis looked around, noting that he hadn't wheeled himself out to see her.

"Oh, he took Farrah to visit with her brothers, and then I believe he planned to tour the newest construction site. You're lucky I just finished up with my last client for the day. I wish you would give us a heads up when you come home, so we can make sure everyone is here. You always just pop in and out at will. If it weren't for the pictures, no one would ever believe we had an older daughter," Martha went on her usual guilt trip of a rant about Genesis never being home.

While Martha ranted, Genesis pulled Gordon aside. "Is the brother still angling to gain custody of Farrah?"

Gordon scowled and nodded. "He got an apartment and made manager at the local box store. I give it another month of visitation before he drops the hammer."

"How is Mom taking it?"

Gordon rolled his eyes and gestured at Martha, who flitted about the kitchen in a confusing back and forth. First, grabbing the charcuterie board, then to the fridge for grapes, then to the pantry for crackers, then back to the fridge for the cheese. The last time she'd been this out of sorts was when Genesis brought up her birth parents for the first time.

"And Dad?"

Gordon went over to help Martha open the jar of olives she struggled with. The fact that he pointedly avoided answering the question told Genesis all she needed to know. Griffin was in denial and probably overworking himself to avoid the topic altogether. Which made sense as to why he wouldn't be home on a Saturday morning and was instead touring building sites.

"Gordon, how's school going?"

"It's school." He shrugged and finished setting up the board while Martha moved on to pulling out a bottle of her favorite white wine. It was barely ten in the morning, another sign of how stressed she was.

One would think a therapist would have a better understanding of how to cope with stressful situations, but Martha had always practiced the do as I say, not as I do mantra.

"Gordon got straight As again this semester, and he's got a little lady friend," Martha gushed, latching on to the much safer topic of conversation.

"Oh really? What's her name, Gordon?" Genesis accepted the glass of wine Martha handed her and took a small sip.

He blushed and shoved a handful of grapes into his mouth.

"Denise, and she's adorable," Martha answered for him.

"So she's met the parents already? That's serious, little bro," Genesis laughed.

"On that note, I have some homework to do," Gordon said and disappeared to his room.

"They aren't dating yet. They were partners on a project together, and she came over to work on it. The way my baby boy showed basic manners was a dead giveaway that he was into her. It made me proud to know all those years of trying to teach him proper etiquette wasn't a waste," Martha said, downing her first glass of wine before filling it again. "How long are you staying this time?"

And there it was again. How could such a simple question carry so much guilt that it weighed like a ton of lead on Genesis's shoulders? The Mabrys had given her everything: their love, their time, their attention, and for the life of her, Genesis didn't understand why she felt it all as a stifling burden.

Maybe it was because she could never tell them the truth. Never show them the real Genesis.

"Two days, then I head to the city to collect the last of my things from Victor's," Genesis said.

Martha scowled at the mention of his name. "I can't believe you left anything with that man-child."

If Genesis was being honest, she could barely believe it herself. Victor was a man-child, one she, unfortunately, liked to fuck on occasion. They had never dated. Romance had never been in the cards, but they cohabitated because it was convenient, and he was always down to test the plausibility of the crazy sex scenes she came up with. Yet, the benefits had quickly been outweighed by the negatives. Especially with him threatening to out her secret identity to the world every time they had an argument.

When she'd left for Sowell City, she'd called his bluff, and since she hadn't heard a peep about Genesis Mabry being Gen Ursa, she at least knew he was more bark than bite. A shock, considering the man's ego usually didn't allow him to back down from a threat, even when it was detrimental to his own wellbeing.

"I locked my room, and I honestly hadn't planned to be gone for more than a weekend, but things happened," Genesis said.

"You're being more vague than usual. Did these things have anything to do with a man?"

Genesis rolled her eyes. "You know me better than that. I promise to elaborate, but later when Dad is here because I don't want to have to repeat it and answer all the same questions over again."

"Fine, but while you're here, please try not to hide in your room on your computer all day."

"You mean like you do?"

"I don't stay in my office all day just for fun. It's work," she said.

"Mine is work too. Anyway, I really need a shower and to box up the few things I left here as well," Genesis said.

Martha frowned. "So, you're leaving us for good?"

The tears were already gathering in Martha's eyes as Genesis rounded the island to give her a hug. "I'm not leaving. I'm just moving someplace too far to justify taking up space here any longer."

"You aren't taking up space. You never take up space. You take too little space, Genesis. I've worked with you for years on this, and you just can't seem to accept that you are worthy of all the space," Martha said.

Genesis sighed. This was yet another conversation they had every time she came home. It sucked because Martha was right. Despite all of their talks and all the love they'd shown her, Genesis still felt outside of the Mabry family. Not because she was adopted, but because she literally wasn't human like they were, a fact she could never share. So instead, she hid away. Kept herself just on the outside of every family gathering and portrait in case her secret finally did what she always feared it would—ostracize her from the first place she'd ever felt comfortable.

"The only mother in the world who isn't itching to be rid of their adult child," Genesis grumbled and walked away.

It was a shitty response, but the only one Genesis could think of at the moment that wouldn't lead to an hour-long therapy session with Martha. Once in the guest room that had once been her bedroom, Genesis relaxed and pulled out her phone. She had the urge to call Baron and hear his voice, knowing that it would help calm her Bear, who paced in aggravation after being kept from roaming for over twenty-four hours. Something that hadn't happened since she'd arrived in Sowell Gate.

"I know your secret," Baron said solemnly when he answered.

Whatever ease Genesis thought she would feel upon hearing his voice was replaced with dread.

"And what do you think my secret is?"

"You're Gen Ursa. Honestly, I don't know why it took me so long to figure it out, Genesis Ursa Mabry."

Genesis's whole body relaxed at his words. She'd been afraid he'd somehow found out about Victor or had come up with some crazy excuse to end things with her.

"Oh, is that all? Well, don't go spreading the news. I hope you understand why I need to keep my privacy on that matter," she said coolly.

Baron chuckled, "Yeah, but tell me, Genesis. How much of what you've written is real, and how much of it is just your wild imagination?"

"You really want the answer to that?"

"I do," he said.

"You want names, places, body count?"

She swore he literally growled into the phone. "No! I just want to know how much ground we still have to cover in your little bag of kink. Fuck, I've been masturbating to your sex scenes for a day and a half. I hope you're prepared for what's about to be unleashed on your ass when you return."

Genesis's whole body flushed with arousal, only partially dampened by the fact that he'd been reading her work. Even after almost twenty published books, along with countless articles, Genesis still had a bit of lingering imposter syndrome. Knowing he was reading her words made her nervous. What if he didn't like her work? What if he hated that she fantasized about Shifter men when he wasn't a Shifter?

"Babe, you still there?"

"Uh yeah, sorry. I just imagined me riding you as you hang halfway off a cliff on a foggy morning," she lied.

"Isn't that a scene from a movie?"

"Obviously, you haven't read that far yet, or you would know my version is way better and way more realistic," she laughed.

"I'll keep reading, but I'd rather have you read them to me. Your words, in your voice, as we reenact every detail," he hissed.

"Are you touching yourself now, Baron? Are you stroking that massive rod of yours to the sound of my voice?" Genesis asked.

"You've surely got some work on your phone. Wanna share what new adventures you've written and join me?" he replied.

Genesis bit back a moan. She would love to phone sex it up, if only she didn't reek of days of travel and wasn't in her adoptive parents' home. Sure, as a teen, she'd explored herself in this very bedroom, but not since she'd officially moved out.

"Actually, I was just about to step into the shower."

"Even better, you can put me on video so I can watch you," he said.

A soft knock on the room door interrupted what Genesis was about to say.

"Let me call you back," Genesis said quickly and hung up. She would have to make it up to Baron later. For now, she answered the door and frowned up at Gordon.

"What do you need?" she snapped.

Gordon rolled his eyes. "Not even home two minutes and already falling back into the bitchy older sister mode. Did I interrupt your little phone call?"

"Yes, you did, so tell me why?"

"Mom wanted me to tell you that Dad and Farrah will be home for lunch. That gives you about one hour to figure out what lies you're going to tell them this time before you go off into the forests again."

Now it was Genesis's turn to roll her eyes. "Don't be salty because Mom outed you about your little friend. Second, I don't lie to them. I just don't give them details, and why do you think I'm going to lie to them now?"

"You're already lying about this being one of your normal visits. Why did Mom say you were taking your things? How far exactly are you moving?" His voice cracked a little as he asked the last question. Gordon's funky attitude now made a lot more sense. He was pissed because he thought she was leaving for good.

With a sigh, she gave her big little brother a giant hug. "I wanted to tell the family all together, but come here," she said and pulled him into the room. She checked the hallway before closing the door.

"So, what's really going on, Genesis? Are you in trouble? Did something happen while you were looking for your birth parents?"

"I'm not in trouble, but yes, something did happen while looking for my parents. Something shocking and completely unexpected," she said with a teasing grin.

Gordon had never liked her penchant for cliffhangers when telling stories, but he sat patiently until she continued.

"Not only did I find my family, but I fell in love. I'm moving to be with my fiancé," Genesis said.

Gordon's eyes bugged out of his head before he picked up her hand and made a show of searching for a ring.

"Engaged but no ring? Where is it? Your purse? Your backpack? Don't tell me you stashed it at Victor's," he said.

Genesis shook her head. "No ring just yet. The whole proposal was kind of an ordeal; we were attacked by a bear, and I thought we were going to die, I thought he was dying, and so I asked him to marry me, and he said yes. I mean, I figured once he got over the shock and the blood loss, he would forget or back out, especially after finding my birth family, but he hasn't yet, so we are taking things slow."

"And why isn't he here with you? How badly was he injured? Why are we just hearing about this bear attack?"

"I told you it was a lot, and this is why I wanted to tell everyone at once."

"You should just lie. Omit the bear attack and the barely fiancé. Say you fell in love with the area while searching for your birth parents. How are they, by the way?"

"Dead, both of them, murder-suicide. I met my father's mother, but she's a crazy cave lady. Haven't searched into my mother's side yet, but I plan to once, you know, things settle down a bit," Genesis rambled.

"So, the note was right. You shouldn't have gone back there," Gordon said.

Genesis shrugged. "I'm glad I went. I knew something tragic must have happened for me to be abandoned the way I was. However, I can't say I regret going. I love the area. Sowell Gate is so beautiful, and Sowell City, while not a huge city, has plenty to offer when I'm not on the mountain."

"And what about this fiancé of yours? Why didn't he come with you?"

"I told him not to. He had a lot of work to do that piled up while he was recovering from the attack. Besides, I promise to bring him to visit once we've figured things out," she said.

Gordon shook his head. "No, you asked him not to come because you like to compartmentalize your life so thoroughly that no one can ever know everything about you."

Genesis was taken aback by her little brother's observation. "I thought Martha was the therapist in the house. When did you get your psychology degree?"

Rolling his eyes, Gordon stood and moved toward the door. "Don't flatter yourself thinking I'd need a degree to decode your secrets when you've always kept a diary or journal," he said before slipping out of her room.

Anger overrode Genesis's shock, but she tamped it down. It wasn't like she hadn't caught him with her diary before, but she'd thought she'd been more careful with her hiding places after that. At least, she hadn't written anything down about being a Shifter herself, but there was still plenty more she had written down about herself, and she couldn't help but wonder just how much he'd been able to learn about her. Of all the family, Gordon was by far the one closest to her. He'd always seemed to know what was really bugging her and did his best to help her in any way he could. Now she knew why. Shaking her head, Genesis closed the door and locked it. She really needed that shower.

Chapter Twelve

Baron sat behind his desk at the Cross Logging office, but instead of focusing on the stack of reports he was supposed to go over, his nose was firmly in another one of Genesis's books. This one was about two Bear Shifter cousins who were into sharing women. He was transfixed at her description of the men sharing the woman with no jealousy or ego between them. Not just in the bedroom but outside of it, in public even, walking the streets, each holding one of her hands. It was fascinating, even though Baron knew he himself could never. He might be too possessive for that sort of thing, but it was damn sure fun to read about.

He was so engrossed in the book that he didn't notice Bechet standing in front of his desk until the book was snatched out of his hands.

"Shouldn't you be working?" Baron looked up to find Bechet scowling down at him. It was poor form to have a favorite sibling, but if there was ever a competition, Bechet was nowhere in the running. As the youngest, he had the biggest chip on his shoulder about the family's history of logging, and that translated into him being a total ass to Baron as the next in line to preserve the Cross Family legacy on Sowell Gate Mountain.

"I'm allowed breaks," Baron said, standing. He reached for the book.

Bechet held the book up and scowled when he saw the half-naked men on the cover. There were two this time, instead of one, representing the two cousins as the male leads. "They've got you reading this garbage too? I swear this has gotten out of hand; even Isis started with this mess."

Baron cracked a smile at that. While he and Bechet didn't agree on pretty much anything, Baron was a big fan of Isis. He didn't mind that she seemed aloof and cold to most people. Baron wished he had her superpowers of making people think they couldn't touch her. In a much smaller capacity than Isis, Baron understood the pressure of expectation and keeping appearances. He was terrible at it, but over the last few years, having Isis around had given him a blueprint on how to handle it a lot better.

"Maybe instead of being your usual hater self, you should try it," Baron said.

Bechet's scowl deepened. "Since when do you call people haters? This is Genesis's doing, isn't it? You might call me a hater, but think of it from my perspective. How many times am I willing to cover for you, to clean up your mess, to play along with the family that everything is fine when your big ass needs much more than a couple casual therapy sessions?"

Baron leaned forward, his face hardening into an angry mask. "Was there a reason you came in here all high and mighty or was it just to run your mouth with some bullshit?" Baron snarled.

Bechet smirked before tossing down the book and reaching into the satchel he wore. He pulled out a thick manila envelope. Baron saw it had Genesis's name written on it in Sharpie. "The background check on your latest honey trap." Bechet turned on his heel and marched out of Baron's office. Which was a good thing because Baron was ready to tear into him for his slight against Genesis.

He didn't slam the door behind him either. No, that wasn't Bechet's style. He was much too put together for anything like that. Instead, he closed the door with a soft click that only infuriated Baron more. Baron grabbed the manila folder and was about to throw it at the door or, better yet, into the trash, but the thickness and heft of the folder made him pause. It wasn't the first time he'd handled information from a background check. If things were simple, cut, and dry, there would only be a few pages, nothing this extensive.

With a frustrated groan, Baron sank back into his chair, the folder burning like hot coals in his hand. How much did he trust Genesis? She'd been full of secrets from day one. Only revealing what she had to. The envelope was Pandora's Box. Once he opened it, there would be no going back. He should throw it in the trash and let his relationship with Genesis happen naturally, with trust at the forefront. But how qualified was he to trust in anyone? He'd been burned before. Bechet hadn't just touched on Baron's insecurities; he'd kicked every single one of them like a pro kickboxer.

Disgusted with himself, Baron tore open the envelope and began reading. His heart pounded in his chest as Genesis's life was laid out before him. He only made it halfway through the file before he took the rest over to the shredder. Guilt wracked him as he reached for his phone. There hadn't been anything in the file that Genesis herself hadn't told him. Sure, there were now details to her vague stories about herself. He now had names, dates, and places. He'd stopped reading right where Genesis had left off in telling him about herself when she moved in with a male friend. He hated Bechet for putting him in this position. He hated himself for taking the bait.

He'd suspected the man was more than just a friend because of how vague Genesis had been when talking about him. Then there was the fact she refused to let him come with her to move her things. Reading about how they met, the circumstances that facilitated her moving in with him, the arrest record the man had—for fighting with a man who got too close to Genesis. That situation didn't sit right with him, and as much as he didn't want to pry, he at least needed to know that she was okay.

Genesis didn't answer her phone, so he called again. No answer. He sat back in his chair and opened the messenger app. He wrote three different versions of messages along the lines of 'call me back, I'm worried about you' and 'I'm sorry I did a background check on you' before giving up with a defeated groan. A message wouldn't be enough. He scrolled through his contacts until he found his cousin Elias's number.

Elias Westmoore, the family lawyer extraordinaire, had helped him immensely through his divorce from Christine. Now he hoped Eli could help him once again.

"Who is Big Bear?"

Genesis nearly jumped out of her skin as she turned away from the box she was packing.

"No one," she said a little too quickly.

Victor scowled at her before holding up her phone to show that Baron was calling. She'd jokingly put him in her phone as Big Bear as a play on his name. He was big, and his name was Baron, Big Bear. She'd also done it just before her trip for this exact reason. She'd followed Gordon's advice about leaving Baron out of the conversation with her parents, and now with Victor, she'd hope he'd see the playful name and ignore it. She gave all her flings play names because they were just for play. Usually, when Victor asked about them, she would give a quick rundown on how good or bad they were in bed. Her silence was more telling than her quick reply.

"Well, 'no one' is blowing up your phone like crazy." Victor narrowed his eyes at her.

Genesis silently cursed herself for leaving her phone in the kitchen. Victor hadn't been home when she arrived, something she'd arranged on purpose. He should have still been at the gallery, setting up the newest installation before the opening in two days. She'd double-checked his calendar on the fridge just to be sure she'd have enough time to have her things packed and gone before he came home and she dropped the nuclear bomb.

She may have not been completely honest with herself about her relationship with Victor. Sure, she liked to think things between them weren't a complicated mess, but it was. She may not have feelings for Victor beyond friendship, but Victor had a possessiveness when it came to her that went beyond a concerned friend. He acted like a single man, didn't throw a fuss about her outside activities or try to manage her life. Yet, every time she'd even hinted about being serious with anyone, he acted out like a jealous lover. This last year, she'd finally realized he thought they were a couple with an open relationship, and they had separate rooms because she snored and he needed his sleep.

Things never should have gotten that far, but she hadn't cared at the time. She'd been too busy trying to figure out who she was to realize anything was wrong until Viktor had made it so she couldn't ignore it anymore. At least, her quest for self had also given her the perfect out. What she hadn't counted on was it also leading her to something good, to someone, to Baron. Genesis reached for her phone, but Victor held it out of her grasp and then had the nerve to answer the call but with video. Genesis rushed over in time to see Baron's happy smile fall as he realized it wasn't her on the other end.

"Good afternoon, Big Bear. Has my Gen's good pussy got you feigning? She should have already told you the deal. Playtime is over. She's back home where she belongs," Victor said.

Genesis's heart nearly stopped beating, and her mouth fell open in shock and absolute terror. Her Bear roared with rage, and the sound came out of her own mouth. Genesis knew there was no stopping the shift that was about to happen. Then Baron spoke, freezing both her and her Bear in place.

"Hello, Victor. It's nice to finally put a face to the name."

How did he know about Victor?

"I see you and Genesis haven't talked yet."

Why doesn't he sound angry?

"Tell her I'll call back later and to just leave her boxes by the door. I've arranged for everything, including her, to be picked up at six."

Then Baron hung up on Victor with a smug smile on his face. Victor whipped around and took in everything, the boxes she'd already packed, the one still sitting open behind her. The way she stood there violently shaking with rage and confusion.

"What the fuck, Genesis?"

Genesis took a deep breath, trying to organize her thoughts before she spoke. At least, Victor had been too focused on Baron to notice her Bear's roar. Her Bear only wanted to focus on Baron and getting back to him, but Genesis knew she would have to handle things here first.

"I'm leaving, Victor. This time for good," she managed to say calmly enough.

Victor stalked toward her but didn't touch her. They both knew that despite his size, she could easily win any fight he started. At least, any physical one. "You were just going to leave and not say shit to me! You think that ugly fucktard is going to give you the freedom I allow you?"

"Allow? Wow, you really got this whole situation fucked up. We are, no, *were* roommates with benefits, Victor. That's all it has ever been for me."

"I can't believe this shit! I took you in. I gave you the space to write your shitty ass bestiality books. I claimed your fat, ugly ass in public, and this is how you do me?"

The urge to let her Bear loose on Victor was almost too much to resist in her anger. Instead, Genesis cocked her head to the side and laughed. "If that's what you really think, my leaving is the best thing to ever happen to you, boo. Feel free to tell your so-called friends that crap so you can save face."

Genesis turned away from him and closed up the box she had been packing and pulled out another empty one. She could feel Victor fuming behind her back. He still hadn't left her personal space and still held her phone in a death grip in his hands. She had a feeling she would be in need of a new one before she got herself and her boxes out the front door. Sure enough, the phone went sailing by her head and smashed against the wall above the headboard of her bed.

"Fuck you, stank bitch. You ain't leaving shit. I'm the one who is done with your ass!" Victor stormed out of her room.

With him gone, Genesis allowed herself to relax, not entirely, but enough to get her things packed in record time. Victor was on the couch, drinking straight from the bottle of his favorite vodka and staring her down as she moved her boxes to the door. She knew she needed to hurry before the liquor gave him courage enough to act again.

"Get ready for the world to know who you really are," he said as she planted the last box at the door.

Genesis rolled her eyes before facing him. "Do what you must. I'm tired of this bullshit, anyway."

He lurched forward in what Genesis was sure he thought was a graceful move from the couch before stumbling in an attempt to get in her face. "I'm going to fucking ruin you. I have pictures and videos of all the dirty shit you're into. You won't be able to show your face anywhere when I'm finished," he slurred.

"I see you want a taste of that jail dick. It's illegal to record someone without their knowledge. Thank you for giving me the heads up, so I can have my lawyer ready. Oh, and I'll also be taking the cost of a new phone out of my rent for this month. Anything else you want to threaten me with before I go?" Genesis made a show of checking the time behind him.

He followed her gaze to the clock. He had about five minutes left before she walked out the door. Regardless of whether Baron had someone waiting for her or not. That was a whole other issue she would have to deal with later. Apparently, he had less time than that as there was a knock on the door.

"I've still got five minutes," he growled.

Genesis smirked and shook her head. "Goodbye, Victor. I wish you the best life you deserve."

She opened the door and was shocked to see Baron standing on the other side.

"You ready?" he said, only he wasn't looking at Genesis. His focus was on Victor behind her.

"More than," Genesis breathed and wrapped her arms around him.

He was so tense, and she knew that despite his outward appearance of calm, she was in for another emotionally intense discussion with him as well. At least for now, her Bear had calmed the fuck down. Baron wrapped his arms around her and gave her a gentle squeeze. She wasn't sure if it was for show or if he was trying to comfort her, but for now, she wouldn't overthink it. She sank into his embrace and took a deep breath, inhaling his woodsy scent that she hadn't realized she'd come to love so much.

"Cute, real cute. Get the fuck out of my house," Victor said and shoved one of her boxes at her and Baron.

Baron moved quick, setting Genesis to the side and getting right in Victor's face. They may have been the same height, but Baron was a good hundred pounds of muscle bigger. Victor being the idiot he was, didn't show any healthy amount of fear at Baron's advance. It was only then that Genesis registered that they weren't alone. A Black man in a suit was suddenly between the two men with a stack of papers that he shoved into Victor's hand. Meanwhile, two movers made quick work of her small stack of belongings.

"Baron, don't make my job harder. Mr. Ross, here is the updated lease for the apartment, along with a nondisclosure agreement about Ms. Mabry's pen name. If you sign these now, this whole incident can be behind us," the man said.

"Who the fuck are you? What makes you think I'll just sign shit?" Victor took another swig from the bottle of vodka. Somehow, he'd managed to hold on to it the entire time.

The man in the suit frowned while Baron made a show of cracking his knuckles. "You are inebriated. I'll have someone come back with the nondisclosure agreement, but you can do whatever you want with the lease. If it isn't signed and returned by tomorrow, you will lose your apartment as the prior lease with Ms. Mabry's name has been canceled. As for the nondisclosure, should you choose not to sign and you disclose Ms. Mabry's identity, there are other non-judicial consequences that may occur."

"Is that a threat?"

"No, Mr. Ross, it's a promise. Have a good rest of the evening."

Genesis stood in the doorway of the apartment, stunned as the lawyer walked out, dragging Baron with him. He motioned for Genesis to come with them, and she quickly followed, no reason to stay behind and deal with Victor's toddler tantrums any longer. When they exited the building, the movers had closed up their truck, and the lawyer talked to them while Baron guided her to a waiting black SUV. The kind that rich people and celebrities usually had, and on second glance, there was a driver as well. Genesis had known the Cross family was well off, but with Baron being as low-key as he was, she'd forgotten that they were also connected. Not just through Bechet's marriage to Isis Hale but through Baron's mother, Melinda Westmoore.

"I'm sorry," Genesis said as soon as they were alone in the backseat. Baron hadn't made eye contact with her the entire time. When she'd opened the door, he'd only barely glanced at her before glaring over her shoulder at Victor, and now, he seemed content to stare out the window.

"Give me a minute, Genesis. I'm still too riled up to have a productive conversation," he practically growled.

She ignored his request. "I don't care. Be angry with me. Yell, scream, whatever. I just can't handle the silent treatment."

Baron turned to look at her then, his eyes blazing, and he grabbed her and pulled her into his lap. "I said I'm not ready to talk, but you obviously need some reassurance about my feelings for you."

Genesis opened her mouth to respond, but he filled it with his tongue. She moaned and melted into him as his hands roughly kneaded her curves. She knew this was not the answer to their situation. Talking would need to happen eventually, but right at that moment, her body and her Bear were all for some angry backseat adventures. If only the lawyer had brought his own ride. The car door opened, and Baron deposited Genesis back into the seat next to him. The lawyer just shook his head.

"I think I'll ride up front."

"No, Eli. We have things to discuss on the way to the airport," Baron said.

Eli looked like he would still rather ride upfront, but he climbed in next to Genesis. "Sorry I didn't properly introduce myself before. I'm Elias Westmoore. Baron's cousin and apparently on-call emergency lawyer," the man said.

Genesis forced a smile on her face. "Nice to meet you, Mr. Westmoore. I'm Genesis Mabry, but you already know that."

"Eli, please. We're about to be family," Elias said.

Genesis glanced at Baron. "I'm not so sure if that's..."

"Genesis, call him Eli, and for fuck's sake, can we stop pretending this isn't a fated mate scenario?"

She couldn't help but laugh. "You really have been reading my books, and what makes you think this is fated?"

Baron rolled his eyes and pulled his shirt collar to the side. "I have the tattoo as proof, and if I needed any more proof, the simple fact that I'm more relieved to have you back with me than pissed off that you lied about being in a relationship when we met, is good too."

"I didn't lie. I wasn't in a relationship. It was a complicated situation. Anyway, fated or not—tattoo or not—you have every right to choose not to be with me."

"If I thought for a second that was an option, I wouldn't be here right now. Now, if you're done lying to yourself about my love for you, I need to finish things up with my cousin."

Genesis gawked at him. "Wait! You love me?"

Baron sighed and took her hand in his before pressing a kiss to her palm. "Yes, Genesis. I didn't want to tell you like this, but yes, I love you. I am in love with you, and if I'm being completely honest, I've been in love with you since the Bear attack."

"I love you too. I've also known since the Bear attack," she laughed.

Baron smiled and leaned in to kiss her. They got caught up in each other once again before Elias cleared his throat. "Sorry to interrupt, but we really do need to do some work," Elias said.

Genesis reluctantly pulled away from Baron and turned a bashful grin on Elias. "Sorry."

He shrugged. "No need to be sorry. Just let me get this done since we aren't far from the airport now."

Genesis nodded and sat back as Baron and Elias handled business. She shot a text to her family to let them know there had been a change of plans but that she would be back to visit them soon. With that done, she paid a little more attention to what Baron and his cousin discussed. Apparently, there was still a lot Genesis needed to know about Baron. They talked about transferring assets, finalizing contracts, and lastly, a prenuptial agreement that Elias presented for her to read and sign. She noticed Elias's nod in approval as she read the document thoroughly and asked questions about wording she didn't understand. It was clear the document was geared toward preserving Baron's assets but also hers as well. She signed just as they pulled to a stop on a private airstrip.

"I guess I don't have to worry about TSA?"

Baron laughed, "Don't get used to private flights. It's a family jet, and Bechet usually has a monopoly on its use."

"Of course, he does," Genesis said.

Elias got out of the car to give them both proper hugs and ask that they come to visit the family in Mulberry soon. Then Baron whisked Genesis into the private jet so he could finally get his hands on her the way he'd been dying to since the moment she'd stepped into his arms at the asshole's apartment.

"Baron, baby, wait. We really need to talk," Genesis gasped between kisses.

"Talk later," Baron grunted as he yanked her pants over her hips and buried his face between her legs.

The last thing he expected was for her to crawl away from him.

"I'm serious," she said, pulling her pants back on.

"Obviously," Baron grumbled, licking the last taste of her from his lips.

"I just want us to be clear about everything before we land and things become more complicated."

"What's complicated about this? We're in love, and we are getting married."

"In the future. Right now, we talk about the past. I know I've withheld things from you. I wasn't intentionally being deceitful; I just like to tell things linearly, and we hadn't gotten that far before I needed to handle some of that past stuff," Genesis said.

Baron had figured as much when going over her background check. He hadn't been lying about being more upset without her by his side than the mess he'd helped clean up for her with that asshole Victor. A mess that still needed a few more passes, with a healthy dose of bleach and maybe some good old-fashioned elbow grease from Baron. He didn't want to think about her being with Victor. All that mattered to him was she was with him now and for the rest of their lives. Still, he couldn't help but ask the one question that still bothered him.

"Were you with him the whole time you were gone? Did you..."

Genesis was back in his lap in an instant. "No! I would never, *could* never, do that to you or anyone else. I went to see my adoptive family, and Victor wasn't even supposed to be at the apartment when I moved my things out. I had planned to leave the face-to-face until the very last minute."

"So, you knew how he would react? Knew he felt he had some sort of claim over you?"

"I suspected that was the case, but Victor and I were never a couple. We were two single individuals who lived together."

"And slept together," Baron said.

Genesis didn't deny the obvious. "Occasionally, yes, but not frequently enough for it to ever mean anything to me."

"That doesn't help."

"I know, but it's the truth. Being a Shifter, our attraction to others is different. Not that we can't feel for others or fall in love, but my Bear was never a fan of Victor, and so he could never have been anything more than a convenience."

"And is your Bear a fan of mine?"

"You know damn well she is, but that's not the point I'm trying to make. I'm trying to properly apologize for dragging you into my mess. I know you went through a lot with your ex-wife, and I didn't want you to deal with any more from me than you already have. That's why I didn't want you to come with me or have to deal with any of this. I wanted to handle it, so I could come home to you without all the extra baggage."

He rolled his eyes. "First of all, if you being a fucking Bear Shifter didn't scare me away, what makes you think anything else would?"

"Because everyone has their limits and their deal breakers. You can't tell me that finding all of this out the way you did, didn't give you pause."

"It did, but then I tried to put myself in your shoes. If the tables were turned, if I was the Shifter, forced to hide who I really was, trying to open up to someone who could never fully understand what it's like. Does it make everything okay? Hell no, but it helps me want to work with you instead of taking it all at face value. Should you have told me about Victor? Hell yes! Would I have handled things the same if you'd told me from the beginning? Maybe, maybe not. I'm choosing to trust you. Choosing to trust in this and knowing what you do about my past, you should know that it wasn't easy to come to that conclusion."

"I do, and that's what makes me feel worse."

"Feel what you must but know this, I love you, and because I love you, I can be more forgiving than I should be, but if you have anything, and I mean *anything*, else you need to tell me, do it now. I can't promise I'll be this understanding if another situation like this pops up."

"You giving me a get out of jail free card?"

"Something like that," he said.

"Well," she took a deep breath, "Victor has photos and video of us together that I didn't know he had until today. And I didn't tell my parents about us because they were too upset by the fact I was moving so far away. I figured I'd wait and introduce you properly when we have a chance to visit again together."

"Wait, you didn't tell your parents about me, like at all? Hold on, let me tell the captain to turn the plane around," he said and reached for the call button on the nightstand next to the bed.

Genesis must have thought he was joking because she shrieked with surprise when he actually made the call. "Baron!"

"Nope, this is happening. I'm meeting the people who raised you and telling them you've met the love of your life. They can't possibly find anything wrong with that."

"Except, they will because as far as they knew, I was with Victor."

"New rule: let's not mention his name again unless it goes along with 'behind bars', 'died in a horrific car accident', or 'fell off a cliff'. It's a damn shame too. I used to love that name; I wanted to name one of our kids Victor but now, nope. The name is stricken from the list."

Genesis shook her head at him before pulling him on top of her. "You were already planning names for future children we never discussed having?"

"I've always wanted to be a father. Have a huge brood to carry on the Cross name. It didn't happen with Christine, and I can only think that it was God's plan for me to only sire a child with my fated mate."

The plane tilted, and the pilot called for everyone to return to their seats as he detoured back to the airstrip. Baron did his best to keep the rest of their conversation light as they headed back to meet Genesis's parents.

Two Years Later...

"You ready to go?" Baron asked, double-checking that all the doors and windows in their home were locked.

Genesis waddled out of the bathroom after having to pee for the fifth time before they made the trip down the mountain to the hospital in Sowell. Genesis had wanted a home birth, but with Baron's past trauma from the loss of his son, she'd agreed to a hospital birth for their cubs.

"Yeah, yeah. Just give me a second," she said, leaning against the couch.

"Just ten steps to the door, another twenty to the car," Baron coached, coming to her side.

Her hospital bag and everything else was already in the car, which Baron had started parking out front just in case. She could do it. She just needed to let this contraction pass. Her belly loosened, and she continued her waddle with Baron's help.

"Did you call Betsy?"

"Yes, she is meeting us at the hospital."

"What about your parents? Are they going to make the trip over the mountain for this?"

"You know they are," he said.

Genesis kept asking questions she already knew the answer to as a way to keep her mind off the increasing frequency and intensity of her contractions. Even her Bear was worried, pacing deep inside. She'd been hibernating for most of the pregnancy, but Genesis waking this morning to her Bear pacing and itching to come out was the first sign she had that her babies would be making an appearance soon.

"Mrs. Cross, if you have our kids on the front steps of this house, I'm going to be pissed," Baron said as he hurriedly locked the front door.

Genesis laughed just as her water broke and splashed across the porch.

"Shit," he cursed.

"I just knew you wouldn't make it down the hill in time," Betsy said, rounding the corner.

"Betsy, don't start. Just help me get her to the car," Baron said.

"Listen here, young man, I like you, but you don't know the natural way. Shifters are meant to be born in the elements, not in no sterile hospital. Now help me get her settled here on the porch."

Genesis thought Baron would put up a bigger fight, but when her next contraction elicited a scream that turned into a Bear-like roar toward the end, he quickly got with the program.

An hour later, Baron was a grinning fool holding two of the three new additions to the Mabry-Cross family. The third rested on Genesis's chest while she caught her breath.

"Told you I would be the one to bring these three into the world," Betsy cackled before packing up her bag. She stayed with them all until the ambulance arrived to take them to the hospital.

"I know things started out rough between us, but I will never regret choosing to have you in my life," Baron said and kissed Genesis's forehead.

"Oh, is that right? Because? I seem to remember a certain bachelor party where you called me, drunk off your ass, saying you couldn't go through with the binding ceremony, even though we had already been married for months," Genesis said.

"Was I not right there waiting for your gorgeous ass at the ceremony?"

"By the grace of God, an IV drip, and the magic of Sowell Sisters' Wedding Planning expertise," Genesis snorted.

Baron scowled, "I thought we were past that."

Genesis was just teasing him. Her way of helping him focus on something other than his nerves about their newborn children. Their ceremony had been amazing and better than she had imagined in her wildest dreams. Not to mention the fact it had become a source of the first real common ground for her and her mother-in-law.

"We are way past that now, buddy," she giggled.

"Keep playing with me, Mrs. Cross, and we'll be right back here with another set of kids," he said and kissed her again.

As her mate cradled her in his arms, Genesis let the joy of the moment overtake her. The road they had taken to get there had been far from smooth, and she'd be lying if she claimed to not have any regrets about the past but, there was one thing she would one hundred percent never regret, and that was Branding Baron.

STELLA WILLIAMS

Stella Williams is a Blogger and USA TODAY Bestselling Paranormal Romance & Urban Fantasy Author, who lives in Washington State. She has a degree in Anthropology from The University of California, Santa Cruz. Stella prides herself in using her studies to create diverse worlds and characters for her novels. You can find more about Stella Williams on her website: www.stellawilliamsauthor.com

Want More of Stella's Seductive Supernatural World?
Keep up to date with Stella Williams and her latest projects.

VIA SOCIAL MEDIA OR NEWSLETTER

**More Books from Stella
Williams**

ALSO BY STELLA WILLIAMS

<u>Sowell Gate Universe</u>
Wild Cross Family

Felling Bechet

Yarding Braxton

Branding Baron

Reclaiming Hunter
Monsters & Mayhem

Peak
Unforgettable Contemporary

Unforgettable Valentine

<u>Maura's Men Universe</u>

Bloodlines

His Soul To Keep

To Catch Akellah
Secret of Ceres

Ferocious

Dauntless

Earnest

Zenith
Langsmith Shifters

Coy Wolf

A Night Divine

Bird of Prey
Maura's Men

Xander's Claim

Claude's Conquest

Shane's Redemption